Dear Bill, Hope that you're feeling better.

all the best

Glenn C. Smith

Tybee Island Terror Plot

Original Manuscript by

Glenn C. Smith

1 Long Marsh Lane
Hilton Head Island, SC 29928-7100
March 19, 2001

Copyright © 2003 by Glenn C. Smith

ISBN 0-7414-1604-2

Published by:

PUBLISHING.COM

519 West Lancaster Avenue
Haverford, PA 19041-1413
Info@buybooksontheweb.com
www.buybooksontheweb.com
Toll-free (877) BUY BOOK
Local Phone (610) 520-2500
Fax (610) 519-0261

Printed in the United States of America

Printed on Recycled Paper

Published August 2003

Statement of fictitious persons
and
Acknowledgements

The story of Tybee Island's nuclear bomb mystery is rooted in truth as documented by The Savannah Morning News newspaper articles that appear in the beginning pages of this work. The story is a work of fiction. Names of the characters and incidents are products of the author's imagination and used fictitiously. The story line and description of the Egyptian terrorists traveling to Savannah, Georgia had its beginning long before September 11, 2001.

Many of the Savannah establishments mentioned in this fictional story exist. The characters are fictitious and the characters identities have been altered or changed to protect any real person.

Thanks and gratitude is extended to the following individuals who assisted with the manuscript preparation, research, important suggestions and commentary; George E. Thibault, Donald W. Nelson, Jr. and Donald P. Scott. Their efforts helped make this story come to life. Many thanks are also extended to my wife, Peggy, for her understanding and helpful suggestions. Thanks are also extended to the Chatham-Effingham Liberty Regional Library for their assistance with historical files, newspaper articles and photographs.

Cast of Characters.

Jack McQuesten; aka, Iron Hand; Navy Captain on loan to CIA, Head of the CIA counter-insurgency team to identify, evaluated and prevent any threats by the Islamic Brotherhood to bomb US mainland targets. Ex–fighter jock, spent four years in Vietnam with the CIA. Commanded destroyers in Newport, RI. Single and looking for the right lady.

Sara Diamond – CIA counter-insurgency team member of Iron Hand's group; analyzes' raw intelligence from foreign operatives relating to attacks against US assets. Computer whiz-kid hacker; specializing in breaking codes and terrorist network security.

George Tilghman – Assistant Director of CIA. Works in the Executive Office Building in White House compound. This office is used to help maintain a perspective different from what one would have if constantly surrounded by the CIA bureaucracy at Langley.

Sherry Norwood – Savannah, Ga. lady who initially learns of nuclear weapon brass ID plate found in Tybee Island waters by shrimp fisherman. Girl friend of Abhul Rahman. 5 Foot 8 inches with a body that stops traffic. Blonde, blue-eyed, Irish/English heritage. divorced from Nick, an ex-Marine; Vietnam vet pot-smoking loser.

Mike Hall – shrimp boat sailor who found brass ID bomb plate in shrimp nets off Tybee Island during routine day of shrimp fishing. First victim of the Arab terrorists in Savannah.

Abdul Rahman – Egyptian professor from Cairo University working in Savannah on middle eastern culture and antiquities for local library and universities. Boyfriend of Sherry Norwood.

Ahmad Rahman – younger brother of Abdul, dedicated Islamic terrorist with strong hatred for America. Member of Osama bin Laden's bomb and terror organization to bomb US targets around the world.

Omar Jamal – Algerian terrorist cohort of Ahmad Rahman. Dedicated Islamic terrorist.

Majed Alnami – Algerian born terrorist; trained in Tunisia and Libya. Demolition expert.

Sergei Bruslov – 34 year old ex-Russian army officer; specialized in handling nuclear warheads for field artillery and Russian air force nuclear warheads. Born and raised in St. Petersburg; grew tired of witnessing the dead and wounded Russian soldiers returning from service in the failed Afghanistan war. Learn to speak English like an American watching TV and listening to rock & roll music.

Captain Rogers – owner & skipper of Miss Thunderbolt; a 58 foot shrimp trawler boat docked on Wilmington River. Crewman found nuclear weapon ID plate while shrimp fishing in shallow waters off of Savannah.

Deane Paulson- Savannah, Ga. native; owned marine salvage & yacht brokering business. Also, former USN jet pilot and wingman for Iron Hand in Mediterranean Sea on USS Kennedy.

Tybee Island Terror Plot

While visiting the Wright-Patterson Air Force museum in Dayton, Ohio retired Command pilot Colonel Robert I. Lagerstrom walked slowly toward a restored B-47 Stratojet bomber. As he stood before the huge jet bomber, his subconscious mind began to drift back to 1959, during the height of the Cold War, when he was stationed in Florida at Homestead Air Force base. As he gazed up at the bomber, he became oblivious to the surroundings as his mind returned to a practice bombing mission flight at 35,000 feet over Savannah, Georgia.

In moments he was lost in reverie of the routine flight that had almost cost him his life and the lives of the two men who had flown with him. He asked himself, "Could this be the very plane I had flown that night?"

For a moment he thought he heard the voices of the flight crew asking him what to do after their mid-air collision with the F-86 fighter. He began recalling details of the night flight that he had long since forgotten. He couldn't imagine it was possible to recall such exact memories that in someway had been buried within his remote memory.

He was transfixed as his mind placed him back in the cockpit, taxiing the huge bomber down the runway to the take-off position. The sound of the six engines winding up for the race down the long cement runway; the last minute preflight check list being read by the navigator, and the flashing green light from the control tower signaling that they were cleared for take-off was vividly recalled. He didn't realize that his wife, standing closely beside him, was staring at him in wonder how this plane had jolted his mind and swept her husband away to another time.

*   *   *   *

February 5, 1958
SAC Air Force Base
Homestead, Florida

The SAC bomber crew had taxied their B-47 Stratojet to the number one runway position for immediate take off. The fully loaded 200,000 pound jet and its sextet of perfectly synchronized GE jet engines were poised to produce 6,000 pounds of thrust when the command pilot pushed the throttle sticks to full power propelling the bomber down the long runway.

"Bombardier to pilot. Final preflight check list completed. Ready for take off."

"Pilot to Control. Flight Romeo ready for take-off. Request clearance."

"Control to Flight Romeo- you are clear for take-off."

"Roger, control," said the command pilot.

The SAC bomber sprang to life, began its forward roll, built up speed roaring down the long runway, and reached out into the darkness. As the bomber climbed into the Florida sky the pilot nudged the plane toward Florida's east coast and steadied up on a northerly course heading. The Stratojet gracefully climbed to its assigned 35,000 foot cruising altitude and leveled off doing 550 knots.

"We'll stay about five miles off the East coast for this mission and our game of tag with the fighter interceptors - if they can find us. The plane is trimmed up and handling perfectly," said the pilot.

The February night sky was clear as the Florida coast began to unfold ahead of the bomber like a lighted road map extending over the northern horizon.

"Navigator to pilot, I compute the time of fighter rendezvous is eighteen minutes at our present heading and speed.

"Very well," said the First Lieutenant pilot.

The Strategic Air Command conducted routine night training missions for its bomber crews under simulated battle conditions by practice bombing targets throughout the CONUS. This constant training was used to sharpen the skills of every bomber crew. Operational readiness training missions were conducted in the spirit that perhaps these crews may be ordered to fly real missions against the European Eastern Block. SAC commanders demanded that the simulated training missions be as realistic as possible.

For this training mission, the Stratojet bomber crew was being ordered to bomb Savannah, Georgia as their primary target, and then proceed farther north to the secondary target, Charleston, SC. The total planned flight time for this mission was four hours. To further insure that the practice mission was realistic, the bomber carried an unarmed nuclear weapon in the bomb bay. Every detail of the training mission was identical to a real mission except, the nuclear bomb wasn't armed and there was no arming device aboard the bomber. The Tactical Air Command had also been advised of the training flight. It was planned that a flight of F-86 fighter interceptors would scrambled and attempt to find the B-47 Stratojet as it practiced its bombing run over Savannah and Charleston.

"I hope these fighter jockeys aren't too aggressive. Sometimes they get cute trying to show us how hot they are." said the navigator. The pilot knew that the navigator always had a comment about some aspect of every mission. There was however, never any doubt about his competence, enthusiasm and interest in the profession of dropping bombs. Dropping bombs and finding women with large breasts were, up to now, his two subjects of expertise.

"Nine minutes until we reach our IP and commence the bomb run on the primary target," said the navigator to the pilot. "Roger," said the pilot.

"Radar picking up a flight of fighters at twenty one miles. Altitude 30,000 feet bearing 270 degrees from our current heading," said the navigator.

"Roger," said the pilot.

"Appears to be four jet fighters in attack formation. Speed 400 knots," said the navigator. "Roger your last," said the pilot.

"Intercept will be in three minutes if we don't take evasive action," said the navigator.

"We are not planning evasive maneuvers or electronic counter measures on this mission. We don't want to confuse the fighter jocks too much. They might ram us.

Chuckle, chuckle," said the pilot.

"It appears that the fighters are being vectored to intercept us by ground radar.

Steady as she goes," said the pilot.

"Coming up on the IP. Commencing bomb run in one minute," said the bombardier.

"Commander, I've been listening to the fighter pilots talking on their radios.

They sound confused. I hope they see us and aren't being too reckless," said the navigator.

"You're right. We don't get paid enough to provide them with any extra thrills."

"I estimate the fighters will attempt to pass underneath us from about 10 o'clock coming from the port side to starboard. The relative closing speed is very high. Less than ninety seconds. Appears that two fighters will be making the first pass, followed by the other two coming in one mile behind the first echelon," said the navigator.

"Commander, I don't like this radar picture. These guys are coming in too fast at the wrong altitude. It's like they don't see us. Hang on to something."

Ten seconds later there was a loud clash of metal scraping metal at a very high speed. The B-47 rocked and pitched to starboard and was out of control for ten seconds. The jet engine blast from the second fighter passed by immediately after the first fighter collided with the bomber and produced a violent sound of the wing tearing and breaking apart. .

"Pilot to crew, a fighter has collided with us on its intercept fly-by. Report any visual damage. I have the bomber under control but our right wing has been seriously damaged."

"Homestead Control from Red Leader on practice mission Sierra Alpha Charlie Romeo. We have suffered mid air collision with a fighter interceptor. Plane under positive control but need immediate landing instructions. Please advise emergency instructions. Over."

"This is Homestead Control. Roger last transmission. We are notifying Hunter Army Air base in Savannah. To contact Hunter punch in on radio frequency six.

They will take over the ground control of the remaining mission. Advise your fuel status and condition of the pay-load? Understand from TAC that the fighter pilot has ejected and his plane has crashed, over."

"Fuel state satisfactory. Pay-load is secure and causing no problem. Our right wing has serious damage. We are losing some fuel from the wing tank. A minor gash in the fuselage is causing excess drag but appears to be stabilized. Request instructions for an emergency landing at Hunter Army Air Field," Over.

"Homestead Control to Red Leader. We have briefed Hunter Army Air base about your pay-load and flight status. They suggest you must drop your pay-load in the sea near Tybee Island. This action necessary to guarantee a safe landing at Hunter. Do you read me, over."

"Red Leader to Homestead Control. This doesn't sound like a good idea but we are not going to argue the point. We need immediate landing clearance. Plane is buffeting and difficult to control. We need a vector to line up for bomb drop. Assume they have us on radar at Hunter. Advise, over."

"Roger your last, Red Leader. Switch over to ground control at Hunter Army Air base. This is our last transmission to you. Acknowledge, over."

"This is Red Leader, Roger Out."

"Bombardier to Pilot. I do not like the idea of dropping our weapon in the sea near Savannah. This payload weighs approximately fifteen hundred pounds and there is no parachute to allow a soft landing. When this bomb hits the water there is no telling what will happen."

"Pilot to Bombardier. My instructions are to get down to 7,500 feet and drop our bomb on a southerly heading at 190 knots air speed. They claim they can find the bomb later by following its drop with ground radar. We don't have time to argue with the Hunter air controllers, or we might be ditching into the sea. Make ready for a bomb drop from 7,500 feet. Out."

"Roger your last, Captain."

"Navigator to pilot – I certainly hope these Army air field guys realize what they have ordered us to do. How are they going to find this bomb in the sea? Talk about devotion to duty. There is no electronic homing device connected to the pay-load to assist any recovery effort when it's under water or stuck on the bottom."

"I agree with you but let's get this thing unloaded and head for the landing strip. Our damaged wing could rip off the plane at any moment," said the pilot.

"Bomb bay doors open. Fifteen seconds until drop," reported the bombardier.

"Bombardier to pilot – bombs away!"

"I sincerely hope no one is down there in a small fishing boat."

February 13, 1958
Savannah, Georgia
Savannah Morning News
Background

Jettisoning of Nuclear Weapons Here Disclosed.
Dumped off Tybee - After Air Collision.
By Wallace Davis, Staff Writer.

A B-47 bomber jettisoned "a portion of a nuclear weapon" in the Savannah Beach area Feb. 5 after colliding with an F86 jet fighter, the Air Force disclosed yesterday. The announcement hastened to add there is no danger of an explosion or radioactivity. A release from the Hunter Air Force Base public information office said the weapons was in "transportable configuration" unassembled when dropped and incapable of detonation.

The release said the Air Force has asked the Navy to help search for the device and that "recovery operations" are now underway.

Savannah Beach residents said naval vessels and a blimp have been active just off the coast for several days. The B47 Stratojet, from Homestead Air Force Base, Fla made a safe emergency landing at Hunter following the midair collision. The pilot of the F86 bailed out.

The Air Force issued a routine report of the mishap shortly after it occurred. No mention was made of the nuclear weapons until last night.

Pictures of the Stratojet taken at the time showed a hole about five feet wide in its right wing and a small hole near the rear of the fuselage. The stabilizer also appeared damaged.

Yesterday's release gave no reason for the jettisoning nor did it give any details about the "portion" of the weapons that was dropped.

Officials refused to elaborate on the release and to answer any questions from newsmen.

The complete text of the statement follows:

"Following the midair collision of Feb. 5 in the Savannah area a B47 bomber jettisoned a portion of a nuclear weapon in the Tybee Beach area. The weapon was in a transportable configuration and not capable of nuclear explosion or radioactivity. The Air Force has asked the Navy to aid in recovering. Recovery operations are now underway."

The term "transportable configuration" presumably means the device was not assembled or armed.

Unofficial sources said the bomber's crew probably jettisoned the "portion" to lighten the plane and increase its chances of landing safely.

Pilot of the fighter ejected himself and landed safely near Estill, SC. His plane crashed in a farm field near Sylvania, SC. An Air Force report said the collision occurred at 35,000 feet.

Yesterday's announcement did not make it clear whether the nuclear device landed in the sea or on land.

One beach resident reported the Navy blimp was dropping strips of red cloth – apparently markers – on Little Tybee Island.

February 14, 1958
Savannah Morning News

Secrecy-Shrouded Hunt for "Weapon" Continues.

Air Force and Navy workers yesterday continued a secrecy- shrouded search for part of a nuclear weapon dumped into the Atlantic off Savannah Beach last week by a damaged jet bomber. The search said to be about 20 miles offshore, was begun without announcement last Saturday and has continued around the clock. It began three days after a B47 Stratojet from Homestead Air Force Base, Fla. collided with a Charleston-based jet fighter plane about 35,000 feet over the Sylvania area. Air Force officials said there is no danger of explosion or radioactivity since the "device" was not assembled and could not be detonated. The Navy was called in to help the Air Force in diving operations.

February 15, 1958
Savannah Morning News

The Navy yesterday issued a news release lifting some of the secrecy surrounding attempts to recover the nuclear device jettisoned off Tybee Island.

The release, from Sixth Naval District headquarters at Charleston, follows:

"US Navy divers and ordnance men, aided by blimps from the Naval Air Station, Glynco, Ga. are continuing the search in waters off the coast of Savannah for a portion of a nuclear weapon jettisoned by an Air Force B47 bomber following a mid-air collision on Feb. 5."

"The scene is approximately 15 miles southeast of Savannah, and about five miles south of Savannah Beach at sea off the mouth of the Wilmington River."

"Additional divers from the Amphibious Force, Atlantic Fleet, are scheduled to arrive at the search area Saturday aboard the USS Bowers (APD-40), Navy high-speed transport which will provide boats for the divers.

"The search and recovery operations are being directed from the Naval Air Station, Glynco, with Lt.Cmdr. A.J. Arseneault Jr., USN, officer in charge of Navy Explosive Ordnance Disposal Unit No. 2, as on-the-scene commander.

"At present, the Navy divers and ordnance men are operating from the USS Penguin (ASR-12), submarine rescue vessel based at Key West, Fla. and sent to the area on Feb. 8. Rough weather has hampered the operation in recent days."

"With Lt. Cmdr. Arseneault on the scene are two officers and 13 men from the Explosive Ordnance Disposal Unit Two, based at the Naval Minecraft Base, Charleston. Five additional EODU-2 personnel are being flown to Savannah from Cedar Keys, Fla. and 14 divers and three officers will arrive in the USS Bowers Saturday."

February 16, 1958
Savannah Morning News

More Data Released By Military

The military loosened up a bit yesterday and gave out a little more information on the diligent search it is conducting for the component lying somewhere on the ocean floor off Tybee beach. The Defense Department in Washington said there were two reasons for pressing the search: One of cost – "It is a very expensive piece of equipment" and "for security reasons" to preserve secrecy of design. And, from the Defense Dept. came a definition of "transportable configuration," the term the Air Force used to describe the condition of the weapon. In military language, "transportable configuration" means, "in a form carried for safety reasons."

From that it was inferred that the military was talking about a weapon from which the triggering device had been removed in order to prevent nuclear explosion.

The search is concentrated in an area about 8-10 miles due east of Little Tybee Island. The Sixth Naval district, with headquarters in Charleston, SC is in charge of the search.

February 22, 1958
Savannah Morning News

Swamp Area Is Now Scene of Nuclear Device Search

A team of 10 specialists is now conducting a search of a swamp area adjacent to Wassaw Sound on the theory that the nuclear weapons jettisoned of the Tybee coast Feb. 5 may have fallen there. The Air Force added, however that "authorities feel certain" the weapon fell into the sea. The search is being conducted because "no reasonable possibility" is being overlooked, the Air Force said. The team of experts is headed by Lt. William R. Green, of Wright-Patterson AFB, Ohio. Meanwhile, the search at sea continued as Navy experts aboard the USS Bowers probed the depths off the Tybee coast. In the next few days an ocean-going tug will bring a barge her to serve as the base of operations for the search.

The Air Force emphasized again yesterday that the weapon, or portion of weapon, was carried in a state of "transportable configuration" and was incapable of exploding.

April 17, 1958
Savannah Morning News

Atomic Hunt Is Abandoned

The Navy's search for a nuclear device jettisoned in the Atlantic off Wassaw Sound Feb 5 was called off yesterday. The unproductive search, which began three days after the "safe" bomb was dropped, led ballistic experts to believe that "the weapon component probably disintegrated upon impact," the Navy said. No comment on the end of the two-month search was made by the Air Force. Three ships, dozens of aircraft and approximately 100 Navy men had conducted the operation in the area under the direction of Sixth Naval District commandant, Adm. J.C. Daniel, who made yesterday's announcement.

The search had been conducted underwater by divers and ordnance experts and on the islands and marsh sections in the area just south of Savannah Beach. A Navy tug, the USS Umpqua, is en route from Charleston to pick up the Navy's YNG barge from which operations have been conducted. It expected to arrive today at noon.

Chapter I

Wassaw Sound, 2000

"Watch out for that net swinging by your head! Look alive!" Captain Rogers yelled. "I'm bringing her into the wind so we can secure the lines faster." Rogers had been the owner and Captain of Miss Thunderbolt for six years. Unfortunately, profits from Savannah shrimp fishing had gone down hill the last three years. As the crewmen secured the last load of shrimp, crewman Mike Hall estimated this load at four hundred pounds.

A buddy yelled, "Hey, Mike, check out that piece of metal in the net." Hall was so busy thinking about a cold beer after work he had completely missed the piece of brass metal hauled out of the water with the load of shrimp. Hall finally grabbed the piece of metal out of the load of wriggling live shrimp and tossed it into a deck box for examination after the catch was iced down.

Miss Thunderbolt had been on the move since 6:30 a.m. and it was time to head back to port. Rogers figured they were six miles from their Wilmington River dock. He moved his 58-foot trawler smartly through the gentle rolling waters and gazed at orange and red sunset. Scores of seagulls flew around the fantail of the trawler looking for a free meal as she churned westerly into the Wilmington River. The temperature had turned cooler but the humidity of the day was still high, probably in the 90's. After years of shrimp fishing Rogers had developed a fine sense for calling the weather and humidity correctly. As the shrimp trawler made its way back to port, Hall and the other crewmen sat braced against the wheel house bulkhead. They began to examine the piece of brass pulled from the net full of shrimp.

1

"Look at these markings and letters. This seems to be some kind of a military description for a bomb or warhead," said Hall. "I wonder where this came from?" said Hall's deckhand buddy. As the trawler moved closer to the dock, the crew prepared to unload the catch at the Charlie Teeple Shrimp Company. Hall pushed the brass metal ID plate into his jacket pocket and pulled the zipper closed.

As soon as their catch was unloaded, weighed out and iced down at the shrimp wholesaler, Captain Rogers paid off the crew. When Rogers paid Hall his wages for the day, he said, "I heard one of the crew say that you found something in the nets. Can I take a look at it?"

Hall dug into his pocket and produced the brass plate. Rogers took the piece of brass from Hall and examined it. It had familiar markings.

"I served 26 years in Uncle Sam's Navy and mustered out as a chief petty officer working with guns and ordnance. I'd bet a month's retirement pay this is an ID plate from a special weapon or an atomic bomb casing. I remember seeing these same atomic energy commission designation markings on our navy nuclear bombs like it was yesterday. Each nuclear bomb has a service ID plate riveted on the bomb casing so it can be carefully inventoried and stored. Nuclear weapons were always moved around under heavy marine guard to where ever they might be needed for a training exercise or wartime emergency and always accounted for by number."

Hall accepted Rogers' comments on face value because he knew nothing about the military service or nuclear weapons. Hall began to handle the piece of brass inside his jacket pocket and figured he would examine it more carefully in his apartment after he used some brass polish to clean up the metal.

Hall's buddies yelled back to him, "Hey Mike, we'll meet you at Tubby's."

"Sorry Captain. I gotta go now. I'll let you know later when I get this bomb thing cleaned up," said Hall.

Rogers looked at Hall as he left and said, "I don't know for sure, but maybe you should turn this thing into the Coast Guard or the FBI. Let me know what you decide to do. I'd like to keep track of it."

Hall and the crew left the dock and headed for their favorite bar on East River Road, Tubby's Tank House. For now the brass metal plate, or what ever it turned out to be, was just an oddity to maybe look at while they drank a couple of beers.

As the crewmen settled around a table, one of his buddies asked, "Mike, are you going to show Sherry your little discovery from the ocean depths?"

"Why would I show this thing to Sherry?" he said sourly. "She doesn't have any interest in this kind of stuff."

"Maybe she'll give us some free beer if you show it to her," Hall's buddy said sarcastically. Another shrimp boat crewmen said, "I've got something I'd like to show Sherry but it didn't come from the sea."

"OK, what's this all about?" Sherry sang out as she placed another draft in front of Mike.

Sherry Norwood was a tall woman at 5 feet 8 inches, long blond hair and a body that stopped traffic when she walked down the street. Her barmaid job at Tubby's Tank House was perfect because the men customers were extra generous with tips when they waited on them. She got along with everyone, but was regarded as a man's girl. She liked sports and could talk your ear off about NFL football and

3

NBA basketball. Sherry graduated from Savannah High, started college, but dropped out after her freshman year because she couldn't stand studying. She fell in love with Nick Norwood and married him after a short courtship because he looked so handsome in his Marine uniform.

After a brief honeymoon at the Jekyll Island Club Hotel, Nick was shipped to Vietnam with the 2nd division. Fifteen months later, Nick came home with an honorable discharge. Soon it became obvious he didn't care about his marriage, the baby on the way, or anything else except drinking with his buddies. Nick claimed he was too stressed out from nightmares caused by his bad experiences in Vietnam. Sherry had attempted to get him to talk about his troubles but, he always said, "It's just to bad to discuss. You wouldn't understand." Sherry hoped he would get over it and settled down and act like his old self again. On more than one occasion, he drank up his take-home pay in bars before coming home.

After six years of a failing marriage, Sherry filed for divorce and told Nick to get out. Sherry was tired of coping with Nick's Vietnam post war stress, drinking and feeling sorry for himself. The last she knew of Nick, he was living back home with his widowed mother and working part-time driving a van around Savannah delivering legal documents. After only a short time, he began getting traffic tickets for running red lights, stop signs and being involved in minor fender bending traffic accidents.

After his last court appearance, a judge suspended his license for six months and fined him $350. Nick called Sherry. "Sherry, baby, please come down here and bring some money to pay my fine. They will keep me here until I come up with the money."

"How much is the fine or jail time? asked Sherry.

4

"I gotta pay the $350 or spend ten days in the clink," said Nick.

"Call your Mother to see if she's got some money. Maybe, I can help her out a little bit," said Sherry.

As Sherry put down the telephone she thought, this is the last straw. Nick was a pot smoking Vietnam vet loser, who couldn't hold down simplest of jobs. At this point she was beyond any tears for Nick. She hoped that Nick's mother would pay his fine in court. She wasn't anxious to spend her hard-earned money. She just wanted to get on with her life without Nick.

On this early evening after the shrimp boats were docked alongside the pier of the shrimp wholesaler, Sherry overheard a shrimp boat deck hand telling his drinking buddies about the brass ID plate he found in a shrimp net. He thought the brass plate contained military bomb serial numbers for a nuclear bomb.

Normally, some object like this would be tossed back into the waters, but the sailor, at the last minute, thought it might be valuable. He planned to polish this piece of brass and see if it could yield valuable information or he might be able to get something for it.

In no time, Sherry knew the shrimp trawler was Miss Thunderbolt and approximately where it had been when Hall found the brass Air Force bomb ID plate. It was common knowledge that boat captains kept detailed logs of the daily fishing spots to record where the largest shrimp were feeding and which were the easiest to catch. As the crewmen continued to drink their beer everyone soon forgot about the ID plate and began talking about women and where they could be found for that evening.

For the last year Sherry had dated a handsome, distinguished Egyptian, Abdul Rahman, who was an associate professor of Middle Eastern culture and antiquities from Cairo University. Abdul came to the US to evaluate Egyptian antiques for several antique shows sponsored by the Savannah College of Art & Design.

Sherry felt the relationship was going well but she held no illusion it would ever result in anything permanent. She thought Abdul was a decent man who spent money freely and was a welcome relief from Nick.

Abdul lived in Cairo with his family and other cities in the Middle East. He had told Sherry that his younger brother harbored strong feeling against America.

Abdul said he liked dating her because, being a blue-eyed, blonde Christian woman of Irish and English heritage she was exotic. Sherry was smart enough to know you didn't build a long term relationship on this kind of attraction.

At Abdul's apartment the next afternoon, Sherry and Abdul relaxed in bed after a session of making love. Abdul lit up his favorite American cigarette, Winston, and listened as Sherry began relating what had happened the day before at work. Abdul was used to hearing Sherry tell her little stories. He did his best to appear interested. This was just a price he had to pay to keep the relationship going.

"Something weird happened yesterday," she said. "Some sailors off a shrimp boat were drinking and passing around an odd piece of brass metal they had found in their shrimp nets. From what I heard, they were dragging their nets not too far from Tybee Island, when they pulled up a load of shrimp and this hunk of metal. They said it must have come off an old Air Force atomic bomb casing from what the Captain thought by reading the military serial

6

numbers. The crewmen let me look at it. It was sort of spooky to hold it in my hand. The letters and numbers looked real official. What do you suppose it was? Why would something like that be in the waters off Tybee Island?"

Abdul said, "I have no idea. People are always dumping things into the sea to get rid of stuff they don't want. If was probably nothing." Abdul took a long pull on his cigarette and gave Sherry and passionate squeeze and kiss on the lips.

After telling the story, Sherry forgot about the drinking sailors and curled up next to Abdul for a nap. Abdul's mind absorbed this story and he thought it might be interesting, perhaps even useful to his brother back in Cairo. Abdul thought back and recalled that during his research about Savannah, he had read of a lost atomic bomb back in the late 1950's.

Perhaps this fragment Sherry was talking about was from that lost bomb. A determined search party might be finally able to locate the missing atomic bomb and its core of U-235. Abdul day-dreamed about the possibilities of locating the lost bomb. What would an old nuclear bomb be worth on today's black market? If the right parties were approached, the money could be huge.

Immediately after Sherry left the apartment, Abdul e-mailed his brother, Ahmad, in Cairo advising him to expect an important letter via the mail. Abdul never sent e-mail directly to his brother but, left messages at an Islamic website chat room, that specialized in cryptic messages for terrorists organizations.

Ahmad checked the Islamic chat room daily for any messages directed to him with hidden references to Egyptian antiquities. During a previous meeting Abdul had been instructed by Ahmad to never send important messages via e-mail since he strongly suspected that American security forces continually monitored all e-mail communication traffic sent to the Middle East.

Abdul was also warned to protect Ahmad's mailing address from falling into the hands of any law enforcement agency. Abdul never liked this cloak and dagger business, but he took precautions and kept Ahmad's mailing and e-mail address in a small file near his telephone for quick disposal if it ever became necessary.

Abdul went to work and composed a serious letter which basically outline the tale Sherry had passed along. He also made mention of the old newspaper accounts he remembered reading about the US Air Force accident over Savannah years ago.

He suggested that one of Ahmad's friends who was skilled in computers might be able to pull up the old story through a web site connection.

Chapter II

Cairo, Egypt

Ahmad Rahman was thirty years old, single and barely supporting himself working menial jobs. Usually becoming bored easily, he quit and moved on to new work. His first job was an apprentice bicycle mechanic during which he remained long enough to learn how to repair motorcycles. He enjoyed repairing mechanical equipment and obtained regular employment however, it did not bring him the satisfaction he imagined for himself. Ahmad's father tried to secure a job for him in a bureau of the Egyptian government but Ahmad told his father,

"Government bureaucratic work was too boring for me." Ahmad was typical of young Egyptians born into the middle class families, but who now turned against their up-bringing and embraced the hard-line radical wisdom of the Islamic clerics who preached hatred of the west and America in particular. Anti-western demonstrations on the Egyptian campuses occurred daily as clerics spoke out boldly about the corruption of Muslim religious ideals at the hands of the western-backed Egyptian President Mubarak.

Ahmad found himself attending more and more political demonstrations. His parents clung to their hope that by encouraging him to find a decent woman he might settle down, start a family and begin a normal life. His parents didn't know that Ahmad's feelings for women were only physical. He was not capable of having an emotional tie with a woman. All of his friends felt the same about women and Ahmad continued to put his feelings about women at the lowest level of his list of priorities. His parents hopes for

9

him were dashed when they learned that he had agreed to attend a three month terrorist camp in the Sudan.

Young men in Cairo like Ahmad would read the al-Majala daily and watch Orbit TV to learn about the latest perceived insults hurled against the Egyptian people by the Mubarak regime. They heard that Egypt was suffering from a slow down in foreign investment and stagnating employment. Even the once stable tourism business was shrinking after several European tour groups were attacked by Islamic Fundamentalists. As the Palestinian al-Aqsa took hold, Ahmad began to think of himself as being like the hot southerly Khamsin wind that always came from the Sahara desert – the divine wind of change that nothing could stand-up against. In his days of attending Islamic demonstrations Ahmad, fortunately, had never been arrested so the security forces had no record to connect him to any rebellious activities in which he participated. His parents prayed daily that Ahmad would not be arrested and sent to jail for the anti-western hatred and Islamic Brotherhood beliefs he held in his heart.

While growing up with his older brother, Ahmad was never content just being the younger brother who wasn't as studious as his brother. Ahmad excelled in all athletics, particularly soccer, but received average grades from his teachers for his academic efforts. Ahmad's father arranged for him to enter a private school in hopes of encouraging him to become challenged and better educated. Ahmad soon met several young men in his new school from Sudan and they turned his mind toward the radicalization of Arab politics and a highly developed hatred for western culture. Soon he was listening to taped lectures by the influential Palestinian teacher in the Muslim Brotherhood, Abdullah Azzam. Along the way Ahmad obtained a copy of bin-Laden's one hundred and eighty page booklet that described the eighteen basic ways a believer could become a dedicated terrorist. Ahmad was never without bin-Laden's booklet.

10

After receiving his brother's letter that alerted him to the nuclear bomb ID plate, Ahmad arranged for a secret meeting with an Islamic Brotherhood associate to describe the possibility of hitting the Americans with one of their own lost nuclear bombs. Although recovery of the lost nuclear bomb in the waters near Savannah was a long shot, it would not be that costly to make the effort. Ahmad thought that with his dedication, finding the lost nuclear bomb and its core of plutonium and uranium 235 would represent a spectacular achievement. The value of hitting the American mainland was beyond calculation.

Several days after Ahmad had spoken to his contact in the Islamic Brotherhood, they invited him to speak at a secret meeting with the leaders of the Cairo cell so he could outline his plan to recover the lost American atomic bomb.

During the early evening auto trip to his secret meeting of Islamic associates, Ahmad anxiously traveled mountain roads to the Mokattam Hills above Cairo.

Ahmad was warned to take precautions that security forces did not follow him to the safe house. Ahmad repeatedly checked his rear view mirror to see if he under surveillance. If he sensed that someone was tailing him he would double back; park on a side street and wait for confirmation that the suspicious car wasn't interested in his movements. Egypt was being managed with draconian emergency laws that President Mubarak renewed every three years during the twenty years of his rule. The Egyptian police, known as the State Security Investigation, or SSI, aggressively cracked down on any Islamic group that was suspected of posing any threat to the status quo.

It was widely rumored that as many as 15,000 men were held in the high security section of the Tora prison complex in South Cairo. Several of these men were close friends of Ahmad. If a member of an Islamic military group was brought before an Egyptian Emergency Court or Special Military Court and serious charges or accusations were against him, it almost guaranteed a long jail sentence.

As Ahmad was making his presentation to recover the lost American atomic bomb, he carefully watched the faces of the men who would soon be deciding if his plan had merit. He sensed they were carefully masking their feelings toward him until he was sent away and they could talk freely. As Ahmad traveled back to his apartment his feelings soared at the possibilities his plan offered. He made a mental note that if his plan was accepted he owed his brother a debt of thanks for uncovering the bomb information.

Long after Ahmad was in bed sleeping, the Cairo cell members remained up working well into the next morning to formulate their message to the London al-Qaeda head-quarters. The Cairo cell leaders enthusiastically endorsed Ahmad's idea and pledged financial and personnel resources for the mission if London chose to embrace the bold idea. Because the plan was so different from the usual attempts to strike at Western targets, they sent an agent to London to explain the concept rather than risk compromise by sending their message through the mail.

Days later, as Ahmad worked at his tourist company job, he learned that his idea had been conditionally accepted. He would travel to London and personally outline the plan to the al-Qaeda leaders. If the briefing went well he would remain in London and begin the basic planning of the mission against the US mainland.

Upon receiving this news, Ahmad was overwhelmed with excitement and he sensed his life had a real purpose for the first time.

Many years ago, Ahmad had visited London with his older brother and father. Now his politics were radically different from those of his father and brother, Abdul. The senior Mr. Rahman was a middle level career bureaucrat within the Egyptian ministry of health and education. His duties called for him to make trips to the western capitals to gain knowledge on how to improve the lives and health of all Egyptians; particularly those in Cairo with its exploding population.

As his sons grew older, Mr. Rahman was anxious for them to see another side of the western world so he arranged for them to travel with him on of his trips.

Ahmad remembered when his father brought him and his brother to the London Mosque erected in 1977 at Hanover Gate, Regent's Park. Its snow white facade, gilded dome and minarets perfectly complementing the roof-lines of the splendid Regency Terraces. All this was in the distant past and actually difficult for Ahmad to recall. His world had changed when he entered the private university in Cairo and began to associate with young political radicals who hated the west and their support of the Israelis.

For his London trip Ahmad dressed in a conservative dark suit and tie in an effort to appear like a Middle Eastern banker or executive arriving at Gatwick airport on routine business. Ahmad used the underground Inter City-Gatwick Express service to get to downtown London at Victoria station. He walked along Grosvenor Place until he came to Hyde Park Corner. Ahmad used several taxi cabs to throw off any security forces that might have been alerted to follow him. His luggage consisted only of carry-on baggage and was easy to manage as he moved around the city.

Ahmad first traveled to Regents Park and walked through Queen Mary's gardens, exited near the children's playground and crossed the Outer Circle to Marylebone road and up to Madame Tusaud's. He hailed his second taxi on Baker Street and rode it for twenty minutes around Hyde

Park and Green Park before being dropped off on Kensington Road for a ten minute walk past the Royal Albert Hall. After stopping to read the Times on a street bench, he darted through some traffic and walked along Exhibition Road to the Islamic Brotherhood's safe house in the area known as Knightsbridge.

Ahmad reached his destination feeling confident that no one was tailing him, and if they had, he had shaken them off. Ahmad stood in front of a large white three story house, he climbed the ten steps to a large front door. The bell rang softly. A masculine voice said, "Please state your name and business." A few moments later he walked through the door and into a vestibule containing dark chests and well upholstered chairs. The floors were covered in deep pile Persian rugs.

Presently two security men entered the vestibule. They searched Ahmad for any weapon or electronic bugging device. Afterward, he was taken to a second floor conference room. As Ahmad sat in the conference room awaiting the arrival of his first contact with an executive of the al-Qaeda, he admired the oil paintings of Arabian horses, arabesque patterns of flowers and some geometric designs. He could only imagine the value of the art work. Ahmad felt the room temperature was a little too cool for his liking. It wasn't uncomfortable, but it added a chill of danger. Everything else seemed perfect down to the recessed indirect lighting. Ahmad sensed a lurking evil and deadly seriousness. One misstep here and someone could wind up dead. This meeting was going to be strictly business. Ahmad said to himself, "Focus, focus, focus. Put everything else out of your mind." With his mental preparation completed, Ahmad breathed deeply and exhaled. As he sat in his chair, he heard a noise to his left. He turned and saw Abu Qutahda walking toward him. Ahmad quickly rose to his feet and smiled.

Abu Qutahda was a distinguished looking man, about six feet tall, with slightly graying hair neatly trimmed with no facial hair or goatee. Abu Qutahda nodded slightly as he extended his hand toward Ahmad. Ahmad's hand was clammy with nervous perspiration. Abu Qutahda's hand was cool and dry. There was no warm grasp in Abu Qutahda's handshake, but just a perfunctory grasping and then a quick release. He motioned to Ahmad to be seated.

Abu Qutahda was born in Egypt into an upper middle class family. He spent most of his adult life in the Egyptian army rising to the rank of colonel in the intelligence service. He retired when he realized his political beliefs wouldn't allow him to serve Egypt after the peace accords with Israel.

"Tell me about yourself and your family, Ahmad," said Abu Qutahda.

Ahmad began nervously speaking about his life in Egypt and raced through many odd details. Ahmad had not rehearsed answers to this question however, he felt he handled it well.

Ahmad then quickly got into the basic elements of his plan to recover the nuclear bomb in American waters. Abu Qutahda listened for another ten minutes and then held up his hand to indicate he had heard enough from Ahmad at this point in the meeting.

Abu Qutahda leaned forward and looked directly into Ahmad's eyes. He began talking in a soft low voice that commanded attention.

"Ahmad, we need you to realize how important this mission will be if we decide to go forward. If it is successfully completed it could cause the rearrangement of several alliances and perhaps bring about the settlement we desire with the Israeli's and their American backers."

Ahmad had no bad vibes being addressed in this manner by Abu Qutahda.

" I believe that I understand how important this mission could be. I only want the opportunity to achieve the results I have envisioned," said Ahmad.

"I'm sure that you do. We have many al-Qaeda contacts in place inside the US who can render great assistance with this mission. You will learn more about them later," said Abu Qutahda.

Ahmad had felt uneasy sitting at the table, but when he heard this statement by Abu Qutahda he relaxed. He tried not to show any outward enthusiasm. To Ahmad if sounded like the al-Qaeda may have already decided to undertake the mission. Ahmad's brain kicked in and snapped back at him: Focus, focus, focus. Don't become over-confident. You do not know if anything has been decided."

Abu Qutahda then began to outline the risks of the mission as he understood them. Risks of being captured by the American security forces were high and, if arrested, there would be little opportunity for anyone associated with the mission to be freed from American jails.

Death was also a distinct possibility due to the slightest errors in judgment. The odds were high that they could be arrested by the well organized American military counter terrorist teams or the FBI.

After about two hours of discussion the house chef finished preparing the evening meal. Roasted leg of lamb with mint sauce, covered with finely ground black pepper and freshly cut rosemary was much to Ahmad's liking. A mildly seasoned side dish of boiled rice and a small green salad completed the meal. Freshly brewed strong black coffee finished the dinner. Little official business was discussed during the dinner; small talk about living conditions in Egypt were debated along with the political positions of various Egyptian leaders.

As Abu Qutahda was finishing his second cup of coffee he said, "Ahmad, this could be your most important mission for our cause. It also may be your last. I hope you have analyzed the risks and realize what you are about to undertake. Our brothers in 1993 who attempted to destroy the World Trade Center in New York City are serving long jail sentences, dead or in hiding with large rewards posted for their capture. We feel this new mission is worth the risks and we chosen several trustworthy, highly trained brothers from Algeria to accompany you to the US mainland.

Abu Qutahda paused to ensure Ahmad understood this undertaking was dangerous and serious. Abu Qutahda continued to describe other members of the team who would be working with Ahmad in the US. He continued to carefully recite the backgrounds of the men from his memory.

"Omar Jamal, born in Algiers and grew up in a home that spoke Berber dialects. He learned to speak French and various Arabic dialects by the time he was a teenager. Several of his older brothers lost their lives during the Algerian war of independence against France. He remember little of his father after his tenth birthday. He drifted to Cairo and attended several schools and in Arab fervor, he joined the Egyptian army. Omar happily drifted into the Arab Intifada against Israel and the United States. He graduated with high honors from several terrorist training camps in Tunisia. While in Cairo, he regularly worshipped with The Grand Iman of Egypt's Azhar Mosque, which preached ways to inflict damage and pain on Israel and its western allies.

A second Algerian brother named Majed Alnami. He attended state sponsored training camps in Tunisia and Libya. His specialty was explosive demolitions."

Abu Qutahda continued describing the final member of the terrorist team that would attempt to explode a nuclear bomb in the US.

"A former Russian army nuclear weapons expert has been recruited and will join the team after the bomb has been recovered. The Russian will evaluate whether the recovered bomb can be reconfigured to use against the Americans.

If possible, the restored bomb may be used to destroy a metropolitan area on the US mainland."

"Of course, you will be in command of this entire mission. Any member of the team not obeying your commands may be eliminated at your discretion. The men assigned to the team understand this and realize the consequences of not following your orders."

Ahmad listened carefully, honored to be in the company of the head of London operations and someone so close to his real hero, bin-Laden. "What guidelines should guide the best use of my brother in Savannah?" asked Ahmad.

"We feel your brother should not be included in any operational action other than to assist you incidentally. The less your brother knows about your mission the better." said Qutahda. "Do you know if your brother believes in our cause as devoutly as you, Ahmad?" asked Qutahda.

Ahmad knew this was a key question and his answer was critical. Qutahda wanted to see how Ahmad would answer and if he could separate brotherly love from the mission. Ahmad sighed, "My brother will do what I ask and he will remain quiet about anything he learns about the mission. I do not feel he will present any problem. He will be an asset for the success of the mission to hit the Americans."

Qutahda weighed Ahmad's answer and said, "Would you sacrifice your brother if necessary to accomplish this mission?" Ahmad settled back in his dinner chair and replied, "Yes, I would sacrifice anyone to accomplish the mission, including myself."

Qutahda smiled.

It was planned that in ten days Ahmad, accompanied by the Algerian freedom fighters Omar and Majed, would arrive in Savannah, Georgia to learn about the missing US Air Force nuclear weapon first hand. In preparation for their trip, the three men shaved their beards, received conservative hair cuts and dressed in western clothes to appear as respectable middle eastern businessmen on vacation.

They traveled with phony Egyptian passports, visas, false Florida state driver licenses, fake credit cards, electronic equipment and large sums of cash, all arranged by members of the London al-Qaeda organization. The phony travel documents were readily available for the right price from Mafia drug smugglers and black market operators in Marseille, France. Al-Qaeda had regular contact with these organizations to facilitate the movement of their agents for their world-wide operations.

The trip to the US was booked through a London travel agency whose clientele were linked to the illicit underworld of drug cartels, Russian money laundering syndicates, dealers of stolen old master art treasures plus wealthy fugitives desperate to move around the world secretly. On several occasions Interpol and Scotland Yard attempted investigations of the suspicious travel agency but were unable to obtain enough evidence to prove any wrong doing in London's Old Bailey criminal court. These type of shadow agency organizations were usually fronts for organized crime operators to launder their illegal money.

The London travel agency had regular access to certain airports in the Bahama Islands whose officials paid little interest in arriving passengers if the large cash bribes were paid in advance. These custom officials would conveniently not be at their posts when private jets arrived; their passengers were waived through VIP lounges to awaiting limousines. Travel from London to Nassau was via Virgin-Atlantic Airways. From there to Little Abaco Island by private jet.

The Little Abaco Island airport near Treasure Cay in the northern out island area of the Bahamas is just large enough to handle the 1990 Lear 35A jet. The plane was equipped with extra range fuel wing tanks, digital radios, radar altimeters, GPS, thrust reverser, drag chutes, Freon air conditioning, color radar and in-flight phone systems. In short, the perfect plane for the mission of delivering illegal immigrants into a position for a fast trip to the US mainland. The plane and pilots were paid by the London travel agency using US currency arranged by a Nassau bank. With large trees surrounding the landing runway the airport was perfectly suited for a clandestine smuggling operation of drugs or passengers destined for the US mainland. After refueling the jet and allowing four hours rest, the pilots and passengers were ready for a discreet nighttime low level flight to a quiet airport north of Savannah, Georgia. During the final approach to the US mainland the plane would be flying at a altitude one hundred and fifty feet.

Hilton Head Island, South Carolina has an airport that afforded a perfect landing opportunity. This airport is unregulated with no control tower, custom office and little police security for private general aviation. Arrivals and departures are normally controlled over the Unicom frequency 123.0 between 6:00am and 10:00pm. The airstrip

20

landing lights remained on all night after the airport personnel closed up shop and headed home. After 10:00pm, little, if any, attention was given to a private jet plane whose departing passengers appeared as tourists arriving late for a week of golf, tennis or fishing.

After successfully landing on the 4,300 foot No. 21 runway and a fast deplaning, all that remained for the terrorist plotters was a quiet fifty minute limousine ride via the back roads of the South Carolina low country to Savannah. As the team loaded themselves and baggage into the limousine, Ahmad began to think about his cover story if anyone stopped them and inquired about their business. He also pictured his brother's face as he reacted to their meeting in Savannah after not seeing each other for years. Ahmad wondered about the US security forces as he realized how easy it was to enter the US, at least so far. Was it possible that they were being led into a trap laid out by the FBI and local police? Ahmad watched the plane taxi to the runway, go to full power immediately, race down the deserted runway and lift into the black sky. Ahmad worried how the mission would continue to play out as the limousine traveled down the dark back roads toward Savannah.

Omar leaned toward Ahmad and asked, "Why didn't the American authorities ask to see our papers and visas?"

Ahmad said, "The Americans are too trusting and lazy. That is why our mission will succeed."

"Praise Allah," said Omar.

Chapter III

Located on a heavily traveled boulevard named Victory Drive in Savannah there is a seedy apartment complex called The Luxcor Apartments. Upon their arrival, Ahmad and his team members quietly registered in this establishment.

The Luxcor apartments catered to clients who want no attention paid to their activities or are down on their luck. There were no questions asked by the front desk clerk when Ahmad paid in advance for three weeks rent. Ahmad was amazed at how tacky the apartment complex was as they walked down the broken tabby walkway that was shaded by huge live oak trees. Cleaning fluid odors permeated the air as the staff of room cleaners worked their way through the buildings.

Actually, the Luxcor was the perfect set up, because it was doubtful if any law enforcement authorities would imagine a terrorist team would chose to live and operate from such busy location. One team member was assigned to constantly remain in the rooms to protect their baggage, clothes and weapons from anyone snooping around to see what could be stolen. For added security, Ahmad never used the room telephone to contact his brother. All telephone contact was limited to using pay telephones in public buildings or shopping malls. After the team was settled in their rooms, Ahmad electronically swept the entire apartment living space, including TV sets, clock radio and the walls to detect any listening device bugs that might have been installed by security forces.

After any meeting was arranged with his brother, a rental car obtained with false ID was used to conduct their business in darkened parking lots near train stations, shopping malls or bus terminals.

At their initial meeting, the first in two years, Abdul was surprised to see the physical change in his younger brother. Ahmad was leaner and had intensity burning in his eyes that betrayed a hatred Abdul hadn't remembered. Abdul loved his younger brother but this was a different person. By any standard Ahmad would qualify as a handsome man. It came as no secret to Abdul that his younger brother probably had many women to pick and chose from. Abdul guessed his brother's good looks added to his leadership skills. Abdul put this new intensity down as the pressure of command and mission stress.

"How are father, mother and our sisters? Are they all well?" asked Abdul.

"Everyone is fine. Our sisters are busy raising their children and having more babies. Mother always wants more grandchildren. She is disappointed that you aren't married and raising a large brood of sons," said Ahmad.

"Sometimes I miss talking with our father and listening to his wise comments about life," said Abdul.

"Isn't it time for you to return to Cairo and settle down. This is our mother's dream," said Ahmad.

"What does father think about you're coming to the US?" asked Abdul.

"He doesn't know I am here," said Ahmad.

"Where does he think you are?" asked Abdul.

"I decided not to tell him about this mission. The less he knows the better if something happens to me," said Ahmad.

Abdul sensed it was futile to continue this conversation about their family. It was obvious that Ahmad had an obsession about his mission and was anxious to get down to business.

"Let's talk about that sailor who found the atomic bomb brass ID plate. Do you know where he lives?" asked Ahmad.

"No, but I know where he drinks almost every night. We can easily find out where he lives by following him home. It will be no problem," said Abdul.

Abdul sensed he was being slowly drawn into situation which he didn't entirely understand. He was uneasy about how it would effect his current life. He didn't mind assisting his brother with a few minor details but he wasn't eager to bring suspicion on himself, get arrested, or be forced to flee the US. Bombing American installations in the Middle East was one thing, but bombing targets in the US was an activity that Abdul had no interest.

The next evening Abdul went to Tubby's Tank House restaurant on River Road to see Sherry. Abdul was certain that Sherry could identify the sailor who had found the atomic bomb ID plate. Abdul seated himself at his usual table next to the wall and near the kitchen. Abdul greeted Sherry with a big smile and said,

"Please bring me an order of raw baby shrimp."

"How many do you want," asked Sherry.

"Maybe a dozen or so," said Abdul.

"Sure, that will be easy. The kitchen staff knows that's your favorite meal," said Sherry. After she placed the order she returned to the table with a cup of hot black coffee.

"Does the sailor you told me about still come here?" asked Abdul.

Sherry looked surprised at the question and said,

"You mean the guy who found the bomb ID plate in the shrimp net?"

"Yes, that's the man. Does he come here anymore?"

Sherry looked around the bar area and said, "You know what. He's sitting right over there in the middle of those guys drinking beer. The bomb fragment is all he talks about. His name is Mike Hall."

Abdul casually looked over at Hall and fixed his face in his memory. This would be necessary so he could point him out to Ahmad. As soon as Abdul was sure he wouldn't forget Hall's face, he finished his shrimp dinner, drank his coffee and, after leaving a generous tip for Sherry, discreetly left the bar. Abdul went to the telephone just outside the building and called Ahmad to arrange for an immediate meeting in Tubby's parking lot. In less than fifteen minutes, Ahmad and Omar arrived. Ahmad immediately joined Abdul in his car and they talked quietly while waiting for Hall to leave Tubby's. Omar left the two brothers alone and drove back to the Luxcor apartments.

In about a half hour later, Hall walked out of Tubby's alone and headed to his old beat up car.

"There's the man who found the bomb fragment. He has been drinking for about two hours. I'm sure he will lead us directly to his place," said Abdul.

"Good work, my brother," said Ahmad.

Mike Hall had been a golden glove boxer of note but he lost too many close fights and never was able to achieve his dream of becoming a big time prize fighter. He closed out his fighting career doing club fights and occasionally got involved beating up a dead beat for loan sharks around

Savannah. Work on a shrimp boat was the perfect job for Hall. He received a daily percentage of any catch and could come and go with the shrimp season. Hall didn't like being tied down a regular work schedule although he had been a bar bouncer until it became boring. When Hall left Tubby's he had no idea that two men were following him.

Hall routinely drove around town after boozing it up with his shrimp boat buddies. He never considered the consequences of being picked up by the police for DUI. As he headed toward his place he sped through several right lights. Fortunately for him, there were no police around to stop him. Abdul had no trouble keeping an eye on Hall since his junk car had a broken red taillight. At the corner of Waters and Derenne Avenues Hall slowed down and parked on the street. Hall soon led his pursuers to a modest three story building that appeared to be well maintained but had little security. Abdul and Ahmad remained in their car and watched as lights came on in a corner apartment that faced the street and alley way which ran behind the building.

Ahmad knew that this building would be easy to enter and search Hall's rooms. Satisfied they had their next objective pinned down, Abdul returned Ahmad to The Luxcor Apartment complex.

Once Ahmad had zeroed-in where Hall lived, he decided to enter Hall's rooms the next day after he went to work. The last thing Ahmad wanted was a serious confrontation with Hall. Ahmad needed the Air Force bomb ID plate that contained military code serial numbers for the nuclear bomb. Possession of these serial numbers would be a key ingredient to make their extortion threat believable. Ahmad was confident he could enter Hall's apartment, get what he wanted, and leave the building without any trouble.

The next morning Ahmad was up at 5:30 A..M. to stakeout Hall's apartment. By noon Hall hadn't left his apartment. Ahmad decided to leave his stakeout position and return after dark and take a chance on entering the rooms whether Hall was there or not. Ahmad was wasting too much time trying to avoid a confrontation.

At 8:00 P.M. Ahmad and his accomplice, Omar, parked their car half a block from the rear of Hall's apartment. Omar stayed in the car for security and also kept open his cell phone line to render assistance to Ahmad if needed. After reaching the apartment building front door and checking the mail boxes, Ahmad confirmed that Hall's apartment was on the ground level, near the rear entrance. This was perfect for Ahmad's exit plan after he completed his search. When Ahmad reached the apartment door he jimmied the cheap lock with his lock pick. Ahmad made a quick tour of the rooms to ensure Hall was gone. He then decided to chance turning on a light. Although it was riskier to turn on a light, searching a lit room would take less time. Initially Ahmad searched the obvious places for the bomb ID plate; bureau and desk drawers, shoe boxes in the closet, gym bags full of old shoes and pockets of jackets hanging in closets. Under the bed were several small boxes filled with old newspaper clippings about Hall, but Ahmad couldn't find what he wanted. Finally, in the back of a kitchen drawer Ahmad found what he had come for. Hall had apparently been polishing the brass plate to bring out the letter markings and serial numbers. As Ahmad was placing the ID plate in his pocket, he heard a key turning and the front door opened.

There was no time to switch off the light and take cover. Hall came through the door and spotted Ahmad coming from the studio kitchen. Hall challenged Ahmad with a verbal assault. "Who the hell are you and what are you doing in my room?"

Hall made a quick fist and moved to land a punch on Ahmad without waiting for an answer. Ahmad side stepped the looping right hand punch and launched an elbow to

Hall's mid section followed by a quick knee kick to the groin. Hall went down and Ahmad finished with a quick killing blow to the back of Hall's neck.

The fight was over in about ten seconds. Ahmad decided to remove the body from the apartment and drop it somewhere. For the next few minutes Ahmad replaced any objects that were disturbed during the short fight and wiped his fingerprints off anything he remembered touching. Fortunately, the fight had not caused any blood to be splattered around the room. When Ahmad was sure that things were back in order he reached for his cell phone, called Omar, and speaking in Arabic said,

"Bring the car to the rear door of the apartment building. Turn off the car headlights but keep the motor idling once you are in position. Keep this line open and tell me when the alleyway is clear of any people."

For what seemed like an eternity, Ahmad waited and finally received Omar's signal that he was in the back alley and clear of people. Ahmad grabbed Hall by the shoulders and dragged his body out the rear door. With Omar, they pushed the body into the trunk and drove off unobserved toward the waterfront alleys in search of a dark place to dump Hall's remains.

There was no question that the body would soon be discovered but, Ahmad wanted to create a crime scene that appeared to be a murder and robbery after a drug deal had gone bad. Ahmad and Omar chose to drop the body near a vacant garage off East Park and East Broad. All the money in Hall's pockets was taken and his pants pockets turned inside out. Hall's wallet was removed, cleaned out of cash and left a short distance away. After this, Ahmad and Omar drove slowly around town for twenty minutes to make certain they were not being followed.

They parked their car in their assigned space at The Luxcor Apartments. Omar cleaned the trunk carefully and then doubled checked inside the car for any signs of the crime.

The next edition of The Savannah Evening News carried a front page story of the murdered shrimp boat crewman whose body had been found at 7:00 A.M. by children going to school. Police properly identified Hall as the victim and said he was employed as a regular deck hand on the shrimp boat, Miss Thunderbolt.

Captain Rogers was quoted, "I was not aware of anyone who carried a grudge against Hall or that he was involved in any suspicious activities that may have contributed to his death." Police reported they had no clues but the investigation would continue. A routine search of Hall's apartment had yielded no clues.

The police encouraged citizens to call and leave a message on the Crime Stoppers tip line if they had any information.

Ahmad read the newspaper story twice to be sure that the police didn't suspect someone else, other than drug dealers, had killed Hall. Ahmad was more than satisfied with his staging of the crime scene. He and Omar had put to good use the lessons learned at the terrorist camps about how to cover up a necessary murder.

Chapter IV

Meet Iron Hand.

Captain Jack McQuesten, known as Iron Hand at CIA headquarters, had served as a field officer in Saigon during the final years of the Vietnam War. His specialty was recruiting, training and controlling counterintelligence agents for action against the Viet Cong and their sympathizers. Prior to his Vietnam duty, he served four years as a line officer on destroyers in Newport, Rhode Island. As the war weary American public patiently waited for President Nixon's secret plan to end the US involvement in Vietnam, McQuesten plied his trade in the jungles of the Mekong Delta.

Even though McQuesten now carried two hundred and five pounds on his six foot three inch frame and his hair graying around the temples, he clearly recalled relaxing in his lieutenant's stateroom aboard ship, reviewing the results of their operational readiness inspection (ORI). His ship had spent three weeks operating in the North Atlantic playing tag with American submarines. They were now nested alongside pier #2 in Newport, RI with three other aging sister ships. The next two weeks their destroyers would remain tied up to the pier to make the ships ready for an upcoming six month deployment to the Mediterranean Sea.

A tap on the door broke his concentration.

"Lieutenant McQuesten, sir. Looks like BuPers has sent you some shore duty orders," said the ship's clerk.

"You've got to be kidding. Let me see that dispatch."

McQuesten scanned the orders, "My god, they're shipping me off to the CIA in Virginia. I'm going to leave sea duty after four years. I don't believe it."

McQuesten instinctively knew that receiving orders to a CIA billet could be an excellent career enhancement opportunity. Just what the Navy had in mind for him at the CIA was a mystery. He had hoped to see some action in Vietnam before the war ended. Perhaps, he thought, these new orders to the CIA would be his ticket to Vietnam. Duty in a war zone always looked good on a serviceman's record.

"Does the skipper know about these orders?" McQuesten asked.

"Yes sir. He received them today in the classified mail pouch and told me to delivery them to you without any delay," replied the ship's clerk.

McQuesten rubbed his face with his large hands and said to himself, "Well at least the skipper wasn't trying to play some little game with him about leaving the ship right after an ORI inspection." McQuesten noticed the orders specified he should expedite his travel to the CIA duty station. Fortunately, there were several new Junior officers already aboard ship that could pick-up the slack and assume most of his duties. This would make an early departure easier on the ship and Captain.

McQuesten had been ordered to report to Camp Perry, Virginia, which is about ten miles from Williamsburg on the road to Norfolk. After spending four months learning the language of the CIA, McQuesten was told to prepare himself for duty in Vietnam developing friendly Vietnamese agents for spy missions against the Viet Cong. After completing the basic training for field agents, which included a strenuous physical training program; defense, disarming, hand to hand combat, killing with bare hands, and personal survival training in the North Carolina swamps for seven days;

31

McQuesten found himself aboard a crowded C-130 transport headed for Southeast Asia.

Lieutenant McQuesten worked out of his quarters at the CIA compound at the Tan Son Nhut airbase near Saigon organizing clandestine missions with his agents.

Most of his Vietnamese agents launched their spy missions from Vung Tau, which was the Navy's swift boat base. Almost all of his agents had brothers in the Army of the Republic of Vietnam (ARVN) and some family members were even part of the Viet Cong. It wasn't unusual for brothers, cousins and uncles to be fighting on both sides in this conflict.

Information flowed back and forth and was traded between the various family members. It was no secret that generous amounts of American cash paid for most of what he learned. McQuesten knew that some of his most trusted agents were marked men with prices placed on their heads by the Viet Cong. If his agents were ever captured or kidnapped by the VC, their lives would be measured in minutes.

Family members did there best to keep themselves informed about what the other side was doing so they could remain alive and healthy.

McQuesten made regular sorties from the swift boat base in Yung Tau around the Mekong Delta into an area known as the Thanh Phu secret zone. McQuesten and his agents were not interested in killing any Viet Cong or coordinating attacks on hooches. They wanted information and attempted to get advance warnings of enemy movements, raids and political meetings. Once this information was developed it would be passed along to the ARVN commanders and their US Army coordinators. Hau Nghia, an area of five hundred square miles, between Saigon and Cambodia had been ceded to the Viet Cong. This was an area that was of major concern to Lt. McQuesten and his band of agents.

McQuesten had learned from his senior CIA briefing officer that the war was not going well. The Thanh Phu zone was full of Viet Cong guerrillas who would fade away in the face of strength and then charge back as soon as the ARVN vacated any area or objective. Enemy strength was however, increasing every week. McQuesten did not anticipate that his CIA tour would end so abruptly with the sudden fall of Saigon.

He had been sleeping in his protected command compound, when Cao Thuong, his trusted south Vietnamese collaborator, rushed into his quarters and hysterically began talking, "Lieutenant Jack, we must leave Saigon now. Double quick. VC and northern army troop units have invaded Saigon. The war is over. We must go quickly to a boat I have prepared for you and my family to escape!" When Cao Thuong talked fast McQuesten thought Cao sounded like a chicken clucking in a farmyard.

"How much time do we have?" asked McQuesten.

"No time for fancy good-byes. We must leave now!"

McQuesten grabbed his .45 colt automatic pistol and several clips of extra bullets, plus all the US currency in his safe that he could stuff into his pockets. This was CIA money he regularly used to pay off Vietnamese agents for information about VC troop movements. He guessed the cash was in excess of $20,000.

Somehow, Cao Thuong had arranged for an old scow to haul his family and McQuesten down the Mekong River to the open sea and, hopefully, rescue by Marine helicopters. While chugging slowly down the Mekong River and deftly maneuvering underneath the Saigon bridges, female Viet Cong guerrillas guarding the bridges began firing their AK-

47 assault guns at boats and barges carrying anything that appeared to resemble escaping Americans. While huddled out of sight under dirty canvas tarps and boxes, McQuesten kept saying his prayers and plugged up the AK-47 bullet holes with anything handy, including $20 and $50 dollar bills.

Luckily, McQuesten had the presence of mind to grab a small two-way single side-band radio as he rushed from the compound and ran down the back streets to the waiting boat. After they cleared the last bridge in Saigon and headed to open sea, McQuesten made radio contact with a low flying Marine helicopter near their bullet ridden scow.

Once they were all picked up and safely aboard the helicopter, McQuesten requested preferred landing instructions as they approached the large aircraft carrier over the horizon.

"This is US Navy Lieutenant McQuesten with CIA operational personnel aboard chopper number 27. We need a priority landing due to a low fuel state and injured personnel onboard this chopper."

"Roger chopper 27. Make your approach from the bow. You are cleared to land on the number 19. USS Hancock, out."

As soon as the pilot landed and all personnel were clear, a group of Marines and sailors pushed the chopper into the sea. All the Vietnamese nationals were immediately searched and taken below for processing and identification. Any pets, chickens, pigs and mascots were taken away from the Vietnamese and disposed of by throwing them overboard. American diplomats, AID personnel, CIA and military brass were taken to the wardroom on the second deck. At the door leading into the wardroom stood a Marine carrying a sidearm.

"That was one hell of an escape from certain death," said McQuesten to the Marine sentry.

"Welcome aboard, Sir," said the Marine.

McQuesten knew his CIA duties were over but he sensed he might yet, one day, find himself working again for the Company. He learned years later, Cao Thuong had obtained US citizenship, settled in Chula Vista, near San Diego and owned a package liquor store. His son had earned an academic scholarship to UCLA.

After taking a liking to life on an aircraft carrier, McQuesten applied for and was accepted into flight training. He was awarded his gold wings and became a jet jockey, flying A4D Skyhawks off carriers in the Mediterranean. After six years in aviation, his eyes gave out and he returned to the Black Shoe navy and destroyers in Newport.

After years of sea duty, combat in Vietnam and flying off of carriers, McQuesten, now a Captain, figured it would be necessary to adjust his usual persona of hard ass mission focus and operational attitude. His new duties at the CIA would involve managing people, developing and administrating plans and learning to cope with the political realities of the DOD bureaucracy.

While seated at a table in the Officer's Club bar in Newport, he ordered a second round of his favorite drink: a double shot of Cutty Sark scotch, soda, a lemon twist and ice. McQuesten remembered that he did some of his best thinking after he had several of these drinks under his belt. Returning for a second tour of duty with the CIA seemed like an excellent way to wind down from his days as a sea dog man of action. Or so he thought.

Chapter V

East River Road – Savannah

Ahmad was anxious to get aboard Miss Thunderbolt. The boat's name was derived from an Indian legend that claimed a lightning bolt brought forth a gushing spring on the western bank of the Wilmington River. The river was one of several that meandered from Wassaw Sound past Skidaway Island back to Savannah and finally meets the Savannah River. Wassaw Sound emptied into the Atlantic south of Little Tybee Island. Usually there are five or six shrimp boats tied up alongside the Thunderbolt Sea Food pier that cater to restaurants and the locals who want to buy fresh sea food. The pier was approximately twelve feet in width and constructed of pine wood boards which were weather-beaten almost white from years of sun, heat and salty air. The length of the pier was just over four hundred feet. Several walk-ways lead from the pier to the parking lot which is entered coming down the hill from East River Road.

Ahmad and Omar approached Miss Thunderbolt. They hailed the man in the wheelhouse, asking if the Captain was hiring crew. They were waved on board by Captain Rogers. He began interviewing them with casual questions to learn if they knew anything about working on a shrimp boat.

"Where are you men from? You don't sound like Southerners," said Rogers.

"We're just drove up from Florida to find work," said Ahmad.

Ahmad's nerves kicked in at hearing Rogers' comment. Omar was glad to let Ahmad to the talking. Omar warily glanced toward Ahmad.

"We worked around Tampa on shrimp boats," said Ahmad. Omar smiled and nodded his head in agreement with this statement.

"We can start working today if that's what you need. What ever you pay is OK. We need work and know how to do the job," said Ahmad.

Apparently, these were the words that Rogers wanted to hear. Rogers didn't like to appear too anxious to hire men for his boat. Rogers decided it wasn't a good idea to talk about the recent death of the crewman, Mike Hall. He didn't want rumors spreading around the docks that Miss Thunderbolt was jinxed.

Rogers stood his ground and shifted his weight to lean against the pilothouse. He looked them over and said nothing for a few moments as if he was letting his mind sift through all the information these two had volunteered. Ahmad and Omar weren't about to walk away. They had to get work on Miss Thunderbolt.

"I have a trip planned for tomorrow morning. I'll be shoving off at 5:00 A.M."

The two men didn't say anything. They were waiting for Rogers to ask for some identification. They were prepared to introduce themselves as Allan and Oscar when Rogers asked for their names. They also had their fake ID ready if Rogers wanted to see something in writing.

"If you guys can be here tomorrow, considered yourselves hired," said Rogers. As Rogers made the offer to hire the two men he looked at their faces to gauge their reactions. There was no glee or excitement – strictly dead-pan.

Ahmad spoke for both of them, "We'll be here at 5:00 A.M."

"Fine, see you then. If there are no problems you can expect to work as long as the shrimp keep running," said Rogers.

Ahmad and Omar were shown lockers below deck to stow any personal gear and extra day clothes. Captain Rogers was used to hiring men on the spot because he knew other skippers along the Wilmington River would pick up anyone who looked half decent and appeared strong enough to handle the rigorous routine of shrimp boat work.

The State controlled the shrimp season to ensure that the shrimp were spawning eggs for the next harvest and the latest crop were large enough. The State would not allow harvesting shrimp that were too small. Workdays started 30 minutes before dawn and lasted until 30 minutes past sunset. Twelve to fourteen hours a day were not uncommon on shrimp boats. Pay was set as a percentage of the catch with meals and bunks provided aboard the vessel. All wages were paid in cash after each catch was sold.

During a normal day of work Miss Thunderbolt would lower her nets six times and the average catch would be three hundred pounds of shrimp. Years ago it was not uncommon to haul in 3,000 lbs. of shrimp a day but those days are gone.

Thanks to the Clinton Administration's policy of allowing foreign shrimp farmers in Southeast Asia to export cultured shrimp into US markets, the cost pressure on the American shrimp industry was enough to bankrupt most shrimp fisherman.

Miss Thunderbolt burned ten gallons of fuel an hour and, with the high cost of fuel, small loads of shrimp were economically not worth the trouble. When the nets were drawn up by winches many small fish, a few big fish, crabs, squid, conchs, sand dollars and horse shoe crabs came along with the shrimp. After sorting out the shrimp the crew pinched off their heads and iced down the catch. Gulls following the boat, looking for any scraps, quickly cleaned up anything that was thrown overboard.

Ahmad didn't plan to work too long before he searched the logbook of recent fishing locations. The first opportunity to examine the logbook came early on the second day. While underway, Rogers said to Ahmad, "I gotta go to the head for five minutes. Can you handle the wheel? Just steer the present course. Steady as she goes, OK?" The five minutes turned into ten. Ahmad gave the helm to Omar as soon as Rogers disappeared into the head. Ahmad had rehearsed what he would say if Rogers returned and he was caught reading the logbook. He planned to say that he was looking for chart information or fuel consumption records. It took Ahmad two minutes to get oriented to Rogers' scribbled log notes. Finally, Ahmad figured out where Miss Thunderbolt was dragging her nets the day Hall found the bomb fragment.

Ahmad quickly jotted down the coordinates from the logbook for that day. 80 degrees west by 50 minutes -- 32 degrees north by 50 minutes. Five hundred yards south of the Tybee Range, flashing green light every 4 seconds. Depth of nets set at twenty eight feet. Bottom condition noted as sandy with shells. Catch: good.

Armed with this information, the charade of posing as shrimp boat crewmen was no longer necessary. After Miss Thunderbolt tied up at the dock and the catch sold, Ahmad and Omar were ready to quit. So as not to arouse suspicion,

Ahmad put on his best imitation of a worn out crewman and said,

"Captain, we can't work for you any more. We are too tired to continue. This work is much harder than we thought it would be. Sorry to leave you after just starting, but we are quitting to look for easier work."

Rogers accepted this explanation on face value. He thought to himself, that his crewmen were leaving faster than he could recruit them. First the death of Hall and now these two leaving him after only two days. Rogers paid them in cash and they left the dock.

Satisfied that Rogers wasn't suspicious about their short employment, Ahmad and Omar headed to their car and planned their next move; which was to lease a boat and search the area using the sophisticated electronic underwater equipment and scuba gear they had brought along from Europe.

Ahmad was satisfied with the mission progress.

Ahmad said to Omar, "Look what we have accomplished. In less than a week we have the bomb ID plate and located the probable location of where the lost bomb might be resting. If we can continue on this pace we will be heroes for the Islamic Brotherhood."

Omar listened, but was not as optimistic as Ahmad.

"So far we have been lucky. The toughest part of the mission lies ahead."

As Omar drove the car back to their rooms Ahmad looked at Omar and said,

"I feel we are on our way to a successful mission. Allah is smiling upon us."

Ahmad now realized that the time had arrived to bring Abdul into the inner workings of the mission. Using his cell phone, Ahmad called his brother.

"Abdul, we need to meet to discuss several important things. Come this evening to the Colonial Park Cemetery at Perry and Price streets. Can we meet at 6:30?"

"Yes. I will meet you then," replied Abdul.

Abdul arrived near the Colonial Park Cemetery well before 6:30. He drove around the area until he saw his brother's car parked along side Price Street. Ahmad was sitting in the driver's seat watching traffic with a bored look on his face. Abdul luckily found a space nearby, and climbed into the front seat of his brother's car. Ahmad wasted no time coming to the point.

"I need your help. The mission cannot proceed ahead until we have obtained three items that only you can get for us. We need a boat from which we will dive and search for the lost bomb – something 40 to 50 feet long. We will need to rent a building in an obscure area to store the bomb after we recover it. And finally, we will need a covered van or truck to carry the bomb from the boat. I will give you all the necessary cash to pay for these items. These things must be rented in your name and your address. Can you handle all this responsibility?"

Ahmad's face was firm and his eyes were penetrating as he looked at Abdul. Abdul knew that he could not refuse his brother's call for assistance. Besides, what harm would be done? As he thought further about these tasks, he asked himself; Why didn't I think of this potentially dangerous involvement before I told him about the bomb fragment?

Abdul said, "I will do the best job I can to help you get what you need for your mission. I will begin immediately to find a boat."

Ahmad said, "I know you will do a good job, my brother. Although we have not started the water search for the bomb, I am very confident we will recover it. After chartering a suitable boat, proceed with the task of acquiring the building. It may take more time for you to find something acceptable. When we find the bomb, I will leave a message on your answering machine and make reference to a new friend for Allah."

As Abdul drove from the Colonial Park Cemetery he began to think of Sherry and other pleasant experiences. He tried not to be preoccupied with the activities of his brother although he knew the next day he would be reading the classified ad section in the paper looking for a large boat and a building. Abdul knew leasing a truck would be a simple matter. Abdul rehearsed his talking points in his mind about why he was leasing a building and renting a boat. It wasn't a good feeling.

As Abdul began in earnest to charter a seaworthy boat that was capable of being used to conduct the search, he soon realized this job wasn't going to be easy. Several prospective boats were rejected because the owners demanded to remain aboard for the entire charter period. This demand, of course, wasn't acceptable and made finalizing several good prospective boat charters impossible.

Ultimately, Abdul chartered a forty three-foot Sabreliner with traditional down East styling, V-hull vessel, powered by twin 435 horse power Detroit diesels, VHF radios, GPS, auto-pilot, radar and a rear swim platform. The boat also had a winch that could haul out 2,000 pounds of dead weight from the stern or alongside.

The boat belonged to a fleet owned by a salvage company that currently had too many boats and too little business. The winch wasn't original factory equipment but had been installed by the salvage company. This winch equipment made the boat perfect for the recovery mission. The boat was named Serious Business.

When Abdul initially visited the marine salvage company seeking a boat for short term charter he discovered it was going to be easy to close the deal. Since money was of no concern, the important thing was that the boat be capable of performing their mission and not look suspicious to any US Coast Guard cutters that routinely patrolled in the waters near Tybee Island.

Ahmad had told Abdul to develop a cover story that he and friends would be scuba diving to search for old wrecks, lost anchors and civil war cannons. Since the mouth of the Savannah River was a hot bed of activity during the civil war, this cover story fitted in nicely with the local southern mentality. Abdul was careful to mention the cover story about hunting treasurer to the boat owner as he agreed to the details about the charter.

After chartering the boat, Abdul made sure it was well provisioned with food, water and beer. The Islamic Brotherhood of believers had no use for alcoholic drinks however the beer would be another part of their cover story to impress unexpected guests. Abdul arranged for dock space at the shrimp boat pier below the East River road. The boat owner of Serious Business brought the boat to the pier. Abdul signed off the final acceptance of the lease agreement to close the deal.

When Ahmad came aboard the boat, he was impressed. Ahmad used his electronic de-bugging search equipment to sweep the boat of any possible listening devices hidden by the security forces. This had become a routine security measure for Ahmad since he had been briefed in London about all aspects of mission security. No bugs were found.

Under the cover of darkness, Ahmad, Omar and Majed transferred all their underwater electronic search gear and scuba suits to their boat. The apartment house rooms were left with only a few pieces of clothing and non-essential items so it would appear that they were still using the rooms. If anything was stolen from the rooms the loss would not cause a problem for the mission. Serious Business would now become their temporary home.

Abdul read in the Savannah paper that a building located near the waterfront, six miles from the East River road pier near the Wilmington River was available. Abdul scouted out the area and decided it was perfect for Ahmad's mission. It was important that the building be located where the truck traffic from containerships moved day and night.

As Abdul drove into the cinder filled parking lot he felt that the building would meet with Admad's approval. There was an old broken sign hanging on the front door, "No Hiring Today." The owner was seated behind a loose-jointed rickety desk in a dirty office that smelled of machine oil and dirt. Trash cans around the office were filled with discarded papers, old coffee cups and pop cans.

"How long do you want to lease this building?" asked the owner.

"One month, maybe two," said Abdul, attempting not to appear too anxious about making a deal.

"What are you planning to use this building for?" asked the owner.

Abdul was ready for this question but he hadn't rehearsed his answer. He was still overwhelmed by the dirt and smell of the office.

"My brother and friends will be scuba diving near Tybee Island for civil war artifacts like cannons and ship wrecks. Anything that is found will be brought here to be evaluated and analyzed," said Abdul.

Abdul knew that he wasn't as big a talker as his brother but he thought he carried off the cover story fairly well. The building owner looked at Abdul for several moments and said, "I haven't read any news about a diving party looking for civil war stuff. Did you get the permits from the Coast Guard and the harbor authority?"

Abdul felt himself start to break a sweat. His mind raced off on a tangent thinking that he may have blown the entire mission with his foolish story. Abdul gathered himself and said, "Oh yes, all that's been worked out long ago. Quite a few people said we'd never find anything."

The owner of the building shrugged, and looked at Abdul.

"I want $4,000 a month for this building."

"I'll pay $5,000 for the first month with an option to rent the second month for $2,500."

The owner jumped up and said, "You got yourself a deal partner. Here are the keys. See you in two months. Nice doing business with you."

At the time of the bomb drop into the waters off Tybee Island, the technology of underwater search and detection equipment had not progressed much further than what was used in WWII. During the 1980's and 90's, advances in research and development by GE and Garrett Electronics for the detection of metal underwater targets was greatly enhanced for Cold war applications. All of this equipment was now available worldwide to the public through sport diving shops and salvage depots for scuba diving enthusiasts.

The team's diving equipment was purchased in London, disassembled and re-packed for their trip to the US.

Ahmad was familiar with this equipment from his training in middle-east militia camps. Small powerful Geiger counters and metal detectors with sophisticated depth measuring components, discrimination and target elimination calibrating dials allowed underwater searches of wide areas to be completed easily. Ahmad had insisted on the best available underwater search gear and wet suits. Their equipment also included a submersible ocean sled to provide the operator with an audible wide sound tone when detection of large metal objects occurred.

Ahmad devised a circular underwater search pattern for their first dive and reviewed it carefully with Omar. Ahmad decided a circular pattern centered around their anchored boat because it allowed the fastest search in depths of 30-40 feet. Majed functioned as a lookout and remained on board the boat to carry out the cover story if the Coast Guard approached the anchored boat while the dives were underway.

"We have entered an important phase of our mission. There can be no slip-ups," said Ahmad.

"If we are successful in finding the lost bomb and lifting it into the boat, how do we get the bomb off the boat and transfer it to a secure location for evaluation?" asked Omar.

"We can't just unload our bomb in plain sight of people around the dock," added Majed.

Ahmad realized the men were correct. That evening he ordered Abdul to purchase lumber and tools to build a skid box to shield the bomb from any observers on the pier. Several large tarpaulins were obtained to cover the bomb loaded skid box to give them added protection from probing eyes.

After receiving his brother's orders via cell phone to purchase materials for a skid platform, Abdul realized he was being drawn in too closely with the terrorist mission. The clawing feeling in his gut continued to get stronger. Apprehension about his role in helping his brother began to ware on Abdul's conscious.

The next day the weather was clear and the sea calm in the Wassaw Sound and Tybee Island. This was perfect weather for their first day of diving for the lost nuclear bomb. As the terrorists pulled away from the pier, Ahmad felt the boat handled well for its age and size. He reminded himself to commend Abdul for his good work.

"If we are lucky, perhaps we can find the lost bomb in a week and send for the Russian expert," said Ahmad.

Omar nodded to Ahmad and said, "Yes, if we have Allah's blessings."

Ahmad steered the boat into the Tybee Island range and cruised at ten knots down the range until it passed the three mile line. At this point, Ahmad brought the compass heading to due south and ran down five hundred yards before swinging back north until the magnetic compass showed the boat was heading due north.

Anchors were dropped fore and aft to secure the boat's heading due north. This would be the point of departure for the underwater search team to begin the expanding circular search pattern. Once the anchors were secure, the correct flags and lights were hoisted to signal passers-by there were divers working near the boat. Majed continued to rehearse his cover story to himself.

Ahmad and Omar dressed in their wet suits and slipped over the side. Ahmad led Omar to the sandy bottom and they began to familiarize themselves with the seabed by executing a modest search pattern around the anchor line. Here and there they came across discarded debris thrown overboard or lost from countless boats; broken marine equipment, old tires and locker boxes littered the bottom. Occasional forms of sea life darted around them as they explored the seabed

Ahmad assumed the bomb initially buried itself deeply into the bottom after its impact with the water. Over the years however these waters had been regularly pounded by variety of violet storms. The bomb might well have shifted its location closer to the top of the seabed instead of remaining deeply buried. It was well documented that Hurricane Floyd in 2000 had caused the sandy bottom near Tybee Island to shift dramatically.

Tides near Tybee Island and the Savannah River can easily ebb and flow nine feet in normal conditions. Ahmad was hoping the shifting of the sandy bottom might have even pushed the lost bomb into shallower waters. If this had occurred, the odds of easily locating the bomb with their sophisticated electronic search gear would be greatly enhanced.

After forty minutes of the orientation dive in the cold waters, Ahmad and Omar returned to the surface and swam to Serious Business. This marked the end of the first day of diving. After checking the weather forecast, Ahmad decided they would spend the night, perhaps the first of many to come, aboard the boat. Anchoring lights were displayed in accordance with the rules of the Intra Coastal Waterways as the plotters had a meal and retired early for more diving in the morning.

After morning prayers to Mohammed: "I witness that there is no god but Allah, and that Mohammed is his Apostle,"repeated five times, Majed watched closely as Ahmad and Omar slipped into the water to renew the search for the lost bomb. This would be their second full day of searching around the boat. Coast Guard cutters patrolling the area hadn't bothered to investigate what they were doing at the anchorage. The three men all assumed their well - rehearsed cover story about being treasurer hunters would hold up so they didn't worry a lot about the Coast Guard.

While Ahmad and Omar searched the bottom forty feet below the surface, Majed busied himself checking anchor lines, cleaning the deck and doing odd jobs on the bridge. Out of the corner of his eye he saw a Coast Guard cutter about 1,000 yards off to starboard slowly executing a turn in his direction. Majed guessed their speed at five knots. Although startled, he decided not to acknowledge its presence until the cutter made its intentions known. He continued to work with the anchor line as he waited for the cutter to make its move. Majed began to sweat. He didn't allow himself to look directly toward the cutter. His personal defensive antennae kicked in. He sensed he was being watched carefully. He was right.

Majed did not know that the Coast Guard had been monitoring Serious Business for the last thirty minutes. The cutter had been aware of them for the last twenty four hours. They had planned to come aboard the boat for a complete inspection.

Due to a Coast Guard paper work foul-up, the cutter crew wasn't aware that Serious Business possessed all the necessary permits and was, in fact, cleared to search in the waters for civil war artifacts. When the cutter was within fifty yards, Majed reacted and acknowledged them by waving and smiling. Majed had been thoroughly coached to act friendly and not do something that might provoke them to board their boat. Majed's nervous smile and tentative wave to the cutter's crew seemed to do the trick.

"Ship Ahoy," rang out from the cutter's bullhorn. "Do you have divers in the water now?"

Majed nodded, "Yes," and raised his hand and held up two fingers. He hoped the cutter would be satisfied and not come closer. From fifty yards Majed could clearly see several cutter crewmen holding weapons and looking directly at him.

The surface waves of the water seemed to be soothing the potential of a conflict as the cutter crewmen continued to watch his every move. Majed tried not to be the guy who blinked first. He feared that at any moment Ahmad and Omar might break the surface and then the cutter would come close alongside. Majed thought, with luck from Allah, Ahmad and Omar would see the cutter from below and stay well away until it left the area.

"Do you have the required permits aboard ship to be diving in these waters?" asked the cutter crewmen.

"Yes, We have all the permits," said Majed. He was careful not to invite them aboard. Majed held his breath. The next person to speak would be the loser.

"Very well," said the cutter crewmen. "Stay on alert for all the local marine weather bulletins."

With this last statement the Coast Guard cutter engines roared to life and moved off smartly as if they had just received orders for something that was more important than checking Majed's diving permits. As the cutter moved away, Majed's body relaxed. He felt an urge to run to the head.

After thirty minutes into the dive, Omar signaled Ahmad he was picking up faint but steady tonal sounds, about thirty degrees left of their current heading. After checking their hand compasses, they slowly swam toward the area that was giving them a steady tone of some large metal object. After about ten minutes the sound was louder and very steady on the pulse induction detector. The trash elimination detector was indicating the metal object was worthy of further investigation.

Ahmad figured they would be soon looking at an old anchor or perhaps a sunken outboard motor that had fallen off a fishing boat years ago. It would be too much to ask for the luck to actually find the bomb on the second day of searching.

Ahmad assumed that the bomb casing was probably gone after the impact of hitting the water from the drop by the Air Force bomber. The inner working of the nuclear weapon that housed the U-235 bullet would most certainly be intact since it was housed in a stainless steel alloy casting which would be impervious to sea water. The only element missing was the arming device that could explode the bomb. Ahmad was expecting to find the steel tamper device and U-235 target rings from the nose cone of the bomb. It is well known that U-238 has a half-life of 4.5 billion years: U-235 half-life is somewhat less.

Ahmad and Omar dug carefully around the area of the strongest signals. They were excited but remained disciplined in their efforts as they realized they most likely had located the lost nuclear bomb that had been the object of so much searching years ago by the American armed forces. They estimated the bomb, now covered with barnacles and assorted shell life, weighed close to seven hundred pounds. Ahmad tied a small line to the unwieldy hulk and released a floatation balloon tethered to the opposite end of the line. The marker balloon rose to the surface. Omar followed the line to the surface and then swam to the boat which was about six hundred yards due east from the marker. Bringing the seven hundred-pound object from the bottom would not be a problem for the stern hoist.

Once Omar was back aboard the boat he said to Majed,

"I am confident that we may have located the lost bomb."

"The Coast Guard was here and talked to me, but they went away. I think they may come back later," Majed said to Omar without reacting to his news that they may have found the lost bomb.

"Go forward to the bridge and be prepared to plot four bearings and record them on our chart. If we are forced to leave this area in a hurry we must know where the bomb is resting. I will signal you when to take the bearings," said Omar.

Plotting the location with bearings was necessary in case the balloon marker was lost due to an accidental bumping by another vessel. Omar started the engines and gradually steered the Sabreliner toward the balloon marker; maneuvering close to the leeward side. Ahmad remained in the water to insure that as the bomb was raised from the bottom, the boat would shield any view from shore. If American security forces were watching their activity, it was important to keep prying eyes on shore from recording the bomb recovery.

After the boat was positioned over the bomb, Ahmad dove to the bottom to attach a steel cable and swivel bolt from the hoist. Slowly the stern hoist began pulling the hulk from its resting place in the seabed. After a slight strain, the bomb was freed from the bottom. It swung gently on the cable as it was slowly pulled to the surface.

When the bomb hulk broached the water, an exhausted Ahmad was pulled aboard. "This is very exciting. I can't believe the Americans weren't able to find this lost bomb," said Ahmad to Omar. "They just quit looking," said Omar.

Ahmad directed the final hoisting of the bomb from of the water and guided it to the deck. Majed and Omar rechecked the skid platform to make sure there was ample protection to the deck if a wave caused the bomb hulk to bounce on the deck too hard. Once the bomb was brought aboard, it had to be secured rapidly and not be allowed to pitch about the deck.

Majed was standing by, ready with tie-down ropes and tarps to secure the seven hundred pound hulk. Omar kept the engines running to maintain enough headway so the boat was not in danger of being pushed into shallow water by tidal current.

Majed became visibly excited after seeing the bomb near the surface. His demolition training in the terrorist camps involved TNT; not nuclear weapons.

"I hope I will learn more about atomic bombs. Perhaps the Russian can teach me about them," said Mejed to Omar.

"If we live through this mission we will all know a lot more about explosives," said Omar. Majed and Omar exchanged looks of approval about their roles in the mission.

With the bomb hulk on the deck, Ahmad realized there was barely enough daylight remaining to safely travel through the meandering channels back to their dock. "I am worried about navigating up the channels in the dark," said Omar, with a fearful look in his eyes.

"We must get out of these waters since the Coast Guard has already checked us out. I'm sure they will be back to talk to us again. We must be on their list of boats to inspect. We need to leave this area," said Ahmad.

Ahmad knew that if they ran aground in a channel and someone alerted the Coast Guard the mission would be finished. Ahmad made his decision; they would return to their dock immediately.

"Omar, start the engines and head for our dock. Majed, plot the course changes and line-up the charts so there are no slip-ups. We are losing daylight," said Ahmad, in a strong command voice. The team jumped into action.

"Going up these narrow river channels in near darkness means we have a good chance of running aground," said Omar to Ahmad.

"We can start traveling slowly up the river channel and by 6:00pm we will be about a mile and half from the dock. If necessary we can use our spot lights to help us go the last few miles," said Ahmad.

"At least by arriving in darkness we will avoid prying eyes that may want to see what we have found," said Omar.

"The sailors and crewmen that work on the pier should be gone and drinking in bars by the time we arrive," said Majed, trying to say something positive.

"Majed, make sure we are displaying the proper night running lights," said Ahmad.

"It will be done," said Majed.

Unloading the bomb in darkness would provide the security they wanted at dock. Ahmad suspected that dock hands from other vessels or just nosy people might be asking about their progress in finding civil war relics. He remained confident that Abdul had been able to contrive a believable story about the wrapped contents of the wooden platform skid. He knew that Abdul could come up with a story that the Americans would accept.

As Omar piloted the boat toward the mouth of the river channels, Ahmad approached the bomb hulk with his Geiger counter and got solid readings that confirmed the presence of radio-active U-235. Majed took a few moments and worked to remove more of the sediment, sea life and barnacles from the bomb hulk.

Chapter VI

London, England

Once the Islamic al-Qaeda organization in London committed itself to the bomb plot mission aagainst the US mainland, it began a search for ex-military personnel in London who might offer their nuclear weapons expertise to a militant group for a substantial amount of cash.

Abu Qutahda presided over the meeting in the Knightsbridge safe house. Seated at the conference table were senior members of the Islamic Brotherhood. Their faces riveted on Abu Qutahda. He spoke with his usual soft voice.

"We must start a search for an ex-military man who has extensive experience handling atomic weapons, shells or warheads. I think our best opportunity is to recruit someone from the NATO ground forces or an Eastern block officer who is willing to sell his expertise. Old loyalties and hatreds cannot enter into the equation," said Abu Qutahda.

"Can we hope to find such a person in London? asked one of the Brothers.

"Yes. There is an active Russian expatriate community here. Many of its members are former army officers who have defected. I believe we could sort-out some good prospects within this group," said another Islamic Brother.

Abu Qutahda listened and said,

"Since we will be sending our new recruit to the US mainland, it is critical that he speaks fluent English. The success of our US mission could very well rest upon the competence and ability of this person. I am authorizing the recruitment process to begin immediately. Put several of our best men on this project. Start with the Russian community. If we don't find what we want there, we can shift our search to European capitals. On one point there can be no mistake: Our organizational involvement must remain secret until we are satisfied we have found the right person."

It was generally accepted that Osama bin Laden was the leader of al-Qaeda, the most feared Islamic terrorist organization, that masterminded the 1998 US embassies bombings in East Africa that killed 224 persons. Although it was widely reported by the media that bin-Laden operated from his Afghanistan hideaway, he was easily able to direct the al-Qaeda by using modern telecommunication equipment and internet linked computers.

Selection by al-Qaeda of a qualified nuclear arms expert, capable of reworking the lost American nuclear bomb was the most critical aspect of this mission.

At a Russian community cafe, which prepared meals from recipes from the homeland, two friends sat at a table chatting about the local news and gossip. One of them began by passing along a rumor he had heard that a Middle Eastern militant organization was discreetly inquiring to find men who had practical military field experience handling nuclear warheads or bombs.

"I would be interested in hearing what these people have to say," said Sergei.

"I believe I can set up a meeting for you," said Sergei's friend.

"Is there a chance these men are undercover agents from Scotland Yard?" asked Sergei, wondering if this could be a sting operation. He raised his eyebrow as he looked into the face of his friend.

"I'm sure they are legitimate. I've been told they are very careful and guarded. The money involved in this deal for the right man could be huge," said the friend.

"Set up a meeting for me, if you can," said Sergei.

Several days went by with no news about the meeting. Then a message was left on Sergei's answering machine. "A meeting has been arrange at ten tomorrow morning at our favorite coffee house. I will introduce you to some men and then leave you alone."

The day of the meeting, Sergei decided to stakeout the cafe for an hour before the scheduled meeting. He was too experienced to walk into a trap set by Scotland Yard or Interpol. He sat across the street at a restaurant that featured sidewalk tables and service. Sergei quietly read a newspaper and kept his eyes peeled for anything suspicious. About 9:45 his friend showed up at the cafe flanked by two men. Feeling satisfied the meeting was genuine, he walked across the street.

The man was Sergei Bruslov.

Thirty four year old Bruslov was one of many Russian officers trained to handle tactical nuclear warheads, bombs and weapons for field army combat missions. In 1998 the ruble had crashed. Many Russian lives, already miserable, were now hopeless. These young officers no longer had any illusions about halting nuclear proliferation or the transfer of weapons technology for mass destruction.

The Soviet Union breakup and the struggle to establish new Russian democratic institutions had also caused corruption in its upper military command levels and severe morale hardships in the junior officer class. Many junior officers had tired of not being paid and not being able to adequately feed their families. Many couples spent their off duty hours drinking themselves into oblivion. Fortunately, Bruslov wasn't married so he worried only about himself. He was acquainted with many officers from his unit who had quit the military forces and sold their skills to the highest bidders. Bruslov felt sure, if a high enough price was paid, some army officers might even sell small special tactical nuclear weapons under their control, as well as the weapons technology they possessed.

During his regular thirty-day army furlough he returned to St. Petersburg to see his aging parents. He loved the city of his birth and while on leave he dressed only in civilian clothes. He often worked with civilian friends guiding tours around the city, sold souvenirs such as lacquered boxes, patruska dolls and other Russian trinkets in the open street markets to western tourists, mostly Americans. Tourists were amazed at his fluent English. Many thought he was an American living in St. Petersburg. All items were sold for US currency. At the end of his furlough period, he usually had accumulated several thousand dollars which he stashed in his parents apartment. Bruslov would not trust any Russian financial institution with his American currency. He only used rubles to facilitate minor purchases within the city or while on army duty.

When he was growing up, his mother had said he could become anything he dreamed of if he worked hard in school and avoided getting into trouble with the authorities. Bruslov possessed a quick mind for mechanical details and foreign languages. His mother encouraged him to master English. Although he loved his parents for their sacrifices, he had no desire to follow their path of marriage, working in a state-owned electric motor factory and living in modest cramped apartments.

When Bruslov completed his second army enlistment period he planned to leave the army and live in London to seek his fortune. He was thoroughly tired of the Afghanistan war, the deaths of so many young men over nothing and the terrible turmoil it had caused throughout Russia. Armed with his US currency bankroll, he left for London confident he could live better in the west.

During his first trip to London, Bruslov found it easy to establish friendship with other Russian emigres who claimed they loathed what was happening in their motherland but were at a loss over what to do. Bruslov listened to their rhetoric but he had no political convictions. He desired money and to live the good life.

It was about this time that he met with two Middle Eastern men who were interviewing ex-military men such as himself. They expressed interest in his background, training and experience with nuclear weapons. It was obvious to Bruslov that one of his expatriate friends had identified him to the men who wanted to learn about him. He made a mental note: Be careful when talking with friends about his army background even if they said they were tired of Russian politics and the Afghanistan war.

Bruslov decided long ago that he would be an independent contractor and a seller of his talents as they related to nuclear weapons technology. He didn't mind being paid a small retainer but he would not accept large payments of cash that bound him to one militant group. He knew his specialized talent could easily be offered in many troubled areas of the world to clandestine organizations that required his technical knowledge and expertise. Several of his new Russian army friends in London were negotiating with the Serbs, Croats and the KLA in Kosova. Rumors were also spreading that several African dictators were searching for weapons of mass destruction and specialists who could train soldiers to use them in the field. There was no need to tie himself to a single group of militants when so many were ready to pay well for his services.

After his initial meeting in the coffeehouse with the two men, Bruslov had two other more detailed meetings with the same men which finally resulted in a contract job offer for Bruslov to travel to the US mainland. During his third meeting, the militant group identified themselves as recruiters for the infamous al-Qaeda.

"Sergei Bruslov, do you understand this mission against the Americans involves great responsibilities and risks from which you may not survive?" said Haji Murad, the recruiter for the al-Qaeda terrorist organization. Bruslov replied,

"I am confident in my ability to pass as an American because of my physical appearance and English language skills. On many occasions in London I have been mistaken as an American. My payment for this work must be agreed upon as follows: an advance payment of $100,000 to be deposited in my bank before I leave London for the US mainland. Upon success of the mission and my return to London, a second payment of a like amount must be deposited into my account. All of my living and travel expenses while performing this mission must be paid by the al-Qaeda."

Haji Murad looked deeply into Bruslov's eyes, sighed, and said,

"Sergei, we understand and agree to your terms. You must now stand by for our orders. Be prepared for an immediate departure to the US. We are awaiting a confirmation message that the nuclear bomb has been recovered."

As Bruslov left his meeting with Haji Murad he considered again the risk he was taking for the $100,000 in advance and another $100,000 upon completion of the assignment. Bruslov had no intention of allowing this job to turn into a personal suicide mission to gain favor for an Islamic cause. Bruslov decided to have a special contingency escape plan if the American security forces were tipped off and uncovered the plot. Bruslov assumed he could easily blend into the American society and work his way through the US, enter Canada and ultimately return to London.

If the mission was foiled by the Americans, his main concern would be getting away from Ahmad and his cohorts without endangering his life. During a previous minor exploit, Bruslov employed a disguise to slip out of a tight spot, avoid the state police and his fellow conspirators. Bruslov decided this type of secret escape plan would serve him well again in case of an unforeseen emergency or mission breakdown.

Bruslov did not sneak into the United States like Ahmad and the other terrorists. He flew via Virgin-Atlantic airways to Nassau, GBI and on to Ft. Lauderdale, FL. A commuter airline was used to travel to Savannah, Ga. He felt that he could become adjusted to the US and get a better feeling for America by traveling alone with a false passport and fake ID provided by the London Islamic Brotherhood. Bruslov chose the alias of George A. Dickinson for his passport and other fake ID that could be used for renting motel rooms, vehicles, storage buildings and tools and materials necessary to reconfigure the bomb.

During the flight to Savannah, Bruslov checked his large suitcase and carried one piece of hand luggage to his seat. Carefully packed inside his carry-on bag was an emergency disguise complete with a hair piece, light weight clothing, hat, rain gear, leather shoes, a second English false passport, fake ID and cash. Bruslov felt the most important item was his stash of US currency which was enough to bribe his way out of danger and into a safe area so he could begin blending into the general society.

As Bruslov departed his plane and calmly walked to the airport lower level to reach the baggage claim area, he paused by a series of rental lockers. He pulled the locker key out, opened the door, inserted the required coinage and deposited his disguise package inside the locker. Hiding the rental locker key would be no problem; as soon as he was alone in his hotel room, he would conceal the key inside the nuclear weapon tool kit until he felt it was necessary to carry it on his person. Just knowing his escape plan was set and in place made him more comfortable about his role in this mission.

While standing near the baggage carrousel Bruslov shifted his position several times to visually check the crowd to determine if anyone appeared to have him under surveillance. His concern was not so much with any airport security police, but with some member of his mission team watching to see if he did anything suspicious. Bruslov didn't see anyone that fit his personal profile idea of a team member who was ordered to observe his movements.

After retrieving his large suitcase, he proceeded to the ground transportation area and found a taxi for the trip into Savannah. Bruslov checked his watch and began to calculate exactly how much time elapsed during the trip to the hotel.

As the taxi proceeded from the Savannah International airport, traveling south on route 21 past the tired old southern neighborhoods, Bruslov's mind drifted back to his younger days of living in old worn out apartment houses of St. Petersburg. Now he wondered, how many young men were anxious to leave these homes in old Savannah for better opportunities.

As the taxi arrived at the DeSoto Hotel on Martin Luther King Boulevard, the taxi driver offered to provide suggestions for dinner or entertainment. Bruslov replied,

"I don't need anything now but in a few days I may be looking for a good restaurant."

The taxi driver handed Bruslov a business card and said, "Please call this number anytime you want transportation in Savannah."

Bruslov thought this man might be useful if a fast departure was required. Bruslov thanked the cab driver and headed up the old brick steps toward the promenade and front doors. The short walk gave him a taste of the hot, sticky weather of the low country. Inside the hotel lobby the air conditioning felt good although the lobby seemed too dark. The huge glass chandeliers reminded him of hotel lobbies he had seen many times in London. The dark carpeting seem too thick but it was comfortable.

Bruslov approached the registration desk and said, "I am George Dickinson. I have a reservation." Bruslov pulled out his false ID and was happy to learn that he was expected. The clerk said, "Welcome to Savannah, sir. We hope you enjoy your stay with us." Bruslov smiled and thought she looked and sounded like a trainee. There were very few people in the lobby.

Bruslov tipped the bellboy to take his baggage to his room. He then made his way to the main dining room. The sign at the dining room entrance said, Welcome to the Magnolia Room. Please wait to be seated by the Hostess. There was no hostess and only a few waiters folding napkins near the kitchen doors. Dinner was scheduled to begin at 5:30. The special for the evening was crab cakes plus fresh vegetables found in season. Sweetened ice tea and pecan pie topped with vanilla ice cream. No limit on coffee after dinner. Price: $21.95

Bruslov turned and walked toward the elevators and paused by several old pictures of the hotel that displayed its former glory and famous guests. As Bruslov waited by the elevator he notice the lobby had six employees and a few bell-hops milling around trying to appear busy. Bruslov thought he would have to appear casual since there was no way these people could not have seen him. He could only hope they had poor memories about the hotel guests.

As Bruslov settled in his room he began the wait for a telephone call from his leader of the mission. In the meantime, he scanned city maps and the telephone directory for addresses of warehouses, garages and small buildings available for rent. He also attempted to learn how close he was to a bus terminal. Bruslov committed the taxi cab telephone number to memory; it was comforting to know he could call a taxi driver for a quick trip if it ever became necessary.

In years past, the port of Savannah had grown into the largest importer of South American mahogany lumber from the tropical rain forests. Ocean container ships steamed up the Savannah River every day to unload vast cargoes. Containers were seen being hauled over the docks and roads leading to warehouses, storage facilities, and holding yards around the waterfront.

After the civil war and until almost the 1960's, Savannah was not hospitable to outsiders, particularly if they were Yankees coming down to start businesses in the city. Many corporations were told to pack up and leave, because the Southern pride of the Savannah residents would rather do without outside investment by Yankee companies than allow them to come in and steal markets and customers.

The people of Savannah would do things their way, or not at all. Many corporate people from the north, found this attitude very difficult, if not impossible, to cope with in the Savannah business community. They learned the hard way that one had to be born in Savannah, or nearby, to get along. Many Yankees came and went back home saying, "We just got tired of fighting the old boy network."

Today, some remnants of the old boy network exist but new attitudes are in vogue and the City of Savannah is open to fresh ideas and the City Fathers have placed a welcome sign out for everyone.

As the evening dragged on with no call, Bruslov went for a stroll through the nearby streets to become acquainted with the surroundings. If forced to make a break for safety from the law authorities, he at least wanted some advance knowledge of how the city was laid out. Bruslov thought it was sloppy procedure for the team to leave him alone at the hotel so long without contacting him.

Perhaps they were testing him to see if he panicked or demonstrated a lack of confidence. As Bruslov walked, he had no pressure to check his back for police surveillance. He became comfortable playing the role of a salesman in town for the first time, using his English skills and listening to the soft southern Savannah drawl in the streets. If his new friends had him under surveillance he would show them the self control of a cool Russian.

Chapter VII

As the afternoon sun dropped lower on the horizon, Omar began to feel the tension knotting in his neck as Majed shouted out the course changes faster. The water depths became critical and it was necessary to double-check the tide tables constantly as they traversed the narrow river channels.

"I'm going to steer right down the middle of this channel," said Omar. Ahmad was watching carefully as the sun began sinking below the horizon. They had at least three miles to travel before they could even see the shrimp dock.

"Turn on the spot lights and train them straight up the channel," said Ahmad.

"Our fuel supply will be adequate but, now I'm worried about the tide running against us. We can lose five feet of water under our keel," said Omar as he sweated out the mental calculations of time, speed and distance.

"If another vessel comes out of the channel there will be a problem just passing it and having enough water under our keel," said Ahmad. By skillfully maneuvering the boat through the channel, Omar was becoming confident he would get his first line over to the dock in another hour. The primary goal was to arrive safely and not go aground with the bomb amidships. Omar refused to believe that he could not accomplish this job. When he saw the pier lights ahead in the darkness he felt some easing of his anxiety about arriving safely.

Abdul could be seen from Serious Business waiting patiently in the parking lot with the rented Ryder truck. In an effort to not draw any attention Abdul stayed well back from the unloading ramp until the boat was tied up and secured. After docking the boat and final preparations were made, the only thing left to do was unload the skid that held the recovered bomb hulk. Ahmad surveyed the pier for activity by people milling around aimlessly. Abdul would not approach the boat ramp until he got an "all clear" signal from Ahmad.

After about fifteen minutes, Ahmad waved to his brother. He was satisfied that it was time to get on with unloading the bomb. Abdul drove the truck to the ramp.

The stern hoist easily lifted the seven hundred pound skid and gently placed it on the dock. A fork-lift truck available to all boats along the dock was used to get the skid inside the truck. So far, this turned out to be a routine operation. Ahmad said to Omar,

"I only hope we can be this lucky when we drive through the city to our rented building."

"Allah is smiling on us," said Omar.

Ahmad's face grimaced and said, "Yes, but it seems too easy."

Once the bomb was in the truck, Ahmad and Abdul drove directly to the Victory Road warehouse. "I began getting nervous about your arrival," said Abdul.

"I know. Delays and waiting will ruin anyone's concentration and upset the timing of the best of plans," said Ahmad, who was starting to relax. Abdul was obviously nervous. He fretted about driving through the tree-lined streets with an atomic bomb in the back of his rented truck. Abdul kept checking in his rear view mirror for the police. He was sweating and it showed in his driving.

"My brother, you seem a little nervous about driving this truck. Please relax. I think that Allah is smiling on us so all will be well," said Ahmad.

"I wish I had as much faith in Allah as you, my brother. I can't imagine what I will say if a policeman stops me for a minor violation," said Abdul.

"Just keep your eyes on the road and let me worry about the police."

To break the tension for Abdul, Ahmad started talking about the boat trip.

Ahmad said, "I can't believe how easy it was to unload the old bomb off the boat under the noses of the Americans."

Abdul replied, "The rental agency people asked me where I was going with the truck. I told them I was moving my furniture into a new apartment."

"Good story. And fast thinking," said Ahmad, as he noticed that Abdul was responding to the conversation. Abdul seemed to be relaxing and was no longer so up-tight.

Ahmad planned to stay with the bomb until it was safely inside the building and ready for inspection by the Russian bomb expert. As they drove along the streets, Ahmad checked his watch and smiled to himself that he had correctly guessed the entire unloading and transfer operation had taken only forty-five minutes.

"One step at a time," said Ahmad. "Soon the Americans will taste what we have in store for them. They will see what it is like to be bombed in their own homeland."

Ahmad was shaking his fist in a display of triumph over his adversities. Abdul stared straight down the street. He didn't make any comment about his brother's statement.

Abdul was exhausted and desperately wanted to get away from his brother and his terrorist comrades. Abdul began to reminisce about their father and wondered what he might say about his two sons in America. The intensity he saw in Ahmad's face reflected from the lights of the on coming traffic kept him from saying what he was thinking.

As soon as the bomb was unloaded, Omar and Majed moved Serious Business to an isolated forward portion of the long shrimp pier and began securing the boat. They shut down the engines, tied off all mooring lines and locked all the cabin doors. Omar double-checked their work to ensure that all was in order before leaving the boat unguarded. As Omar left the pier walking slowly up the ramp to the waiting car, he looked over his shoulder to see if any security police or snooping by-standers were milling near Serious Business. Satisfied that all was well, Omar ducked into the car driven by Majed and they drove down East River Road to the warehouse.

Omar looked at Majed and said,

"This has been a very successful day for our cause. I hope the rest of our days go this smoothly." Majed looked back at Omar, smiled and nodded his head in agreement.

Abdul drove into the cinder-covered parking lot. Ahmad pressed the electronic door opener and the overhead doors swung open. Abdul easily drove the truck directly into the building and turned off the engine. Relief came over Abdul's body. He let out a huge sigh. Ahmad jumped out of the front seat, pulled down the overhead doors, closed and locked them. They then waited fifteen minutes, until Omar and Majed arrived, before beginning to unload the truck. Nothing was said between the two brothers. They were both lost in their own thoughts.

Ahmad used his cell phone to call the DeSoto Hotel and set up a pick-up time for Bruslov. "Go to the basement parking garage in one hour. I will be standing at the rear of a car reading a newspaper. Be prepared to exchange our prearranged greetings," said Ahmad.

The telephone line went dead. Bruslov sensed his team leader's abruptness was a put-on to appear dynamic and tough. Bruslov had seen this type of behavior by his commanders in the Russian army.

Before leaving London, Ahmad was given a photo of Bruslov to identify him properly when the two men met. Meeting in the basement parking garage was in keeping with Ahmad's practice of avoiding meeting in well-lighted places like hotel lobbies.

Fifty-five minutes later, Bruslov went down the elevator to the hotel basement parking garage. He pushed the hotel luggage dolly along loaded with his personal luggage and a large suitcase filled with the tools of his trade. Bruslov spotted a man leaning on the back of a car about fifty feet from the elevator. As he approached the person he said in a clear voice, "The weather is cooler in London."

Ahmad recited the prearranged response that Abu Qutahda had set up,

"Yes, but only in the Spring."

After a momentary sizing up by each man of the other, they walked along a row of cars until they came to where Abdul was waiting in his car. Abdul heard three soft taps on the back door window. He turned and saw his brother and a man who looked very much like an American standing by the car. For a moment, Abdul thought there was trouble. He released the door and trunk locks. Bruslov loaded his luggage and suitcase into the trunk. The two men climbed into the back seat.

Abdul turned and looked at his brother.

"Abdul, meet Sergei Bruslov.

In perfect English, Bruslov said, "How do you do."

So far, so good, thought Bruslov, as he settled back and listened to Ahmad outline the next phase of the mission. "Oh my god, not more Islamic B.S., I just got here," thought Bruslov.

Ahmad launched into an energetic pep-talk about the Islamic cause and how he demanded discipline. Abdul suspected that his new acquaintance, Bruslov, was lost in his own thoughts as Ahmad spoke about the importance of complete dedication and attention to the smallest details. For Abdul, his only wish was to finish this whole affair, so that he could get back to his former life. As Abdul leaned back to look at the two men he thought he saw Bruslov's eyes starting to glaze over.

Ahmad finally finished his talk and signaled Abdul to drive to the warehouse. It had not been difficult to arrange a favorable short-term lease with all the equipment remaining in the building, including fork-lift trucks, welding equipment and several overhead chain hoist lifts powered by small electrical motors. Abdul had paid the first month's rent with funds provided by Ahmad. He also hired a locksmith to immediately change all the door locks and install new pad locks on the doors.

Once the team was in place, the bomb was given a cursory examination by Bruslov. Ahmad approached the Russian and said,

"I am interested to hear what you think about our discovery from the ocean depths. Do you think it can be reconfigured and made into a weapon?"

Bruslov looked at the hulk and said, "I will have a better opinion after examining what is obviously a large mess. Many of the component parts seem to be missing but the bomb casing for the U-235 plutonium apparently is intact."

Bruslov now realized that he had a virtually impossible task confronting him, but he also knew that Ahmad, wasn't going to accept any lame excuses after all their efforts getting this far along in the mission to blackmail the US government.

While Bruslov continued to examine the bomb, Ahmad rallied his men.

"We must search this building for any listening devices or surveillance bugs left behind by the owner." This action was routine and expected by now.

Although Bruslov was not asked for his opinion, he volunteered, "I feel this building is perfect for our work because of its size and equipment that is available."

This was Bruslov's way of showing Ahmad that he was going to be a good team player. Actually, all Bruslov could think about at this time was putting the bomb into some kind of working order and getting away from these men as quickly as possible. He would play the good team player role until he was ready to make a break from these Islamic Brotherhood fanatics. There was something about these crude men that he didn't like. They seemed worse than his Russian army cohorts.

In the morning, as an additional precaution, Ahmad told the men he wanted every building window painted with black paint to eliminate any opportunity for outsiders to peer inside. Crude living quarters and sleeping bunks were assembled for the men who would stand guard around the clock in the building while Bruslov worked on the bomb. Several old refrigerators were available to store food. A stained sink with hot and cold water was used for modest food preparation. It was soon decided, unanimously by the terrorists, that all meals would be ordered from a nearby fast-food delivery restaurant. Ordering food delivered for each meal could create a situation that might lead to a security breach, but the terrorists had to eat and none of them was capable of cooking an edible meal.

Bruslov was designated to be the contact man to order their meals and pay the deliveryman. This was so ordered because he looked like an American and spoke English so well. This would also cut down on snooping by delivery people when their meals arrived.

After the bomb was unloaded and the final cleaning up was accomplished, Bruslov, went to work examining what had to be done. He began work on the inner core of U-235 with his instruments and timing devices.

After his first examination of the stainless steel casement Bruslov said,

"Here are several serial ID numbers I found that were welded to the U-235 casing. Perhaps, they will aid you in convincing the Americans we have one of their old atomic bombs."

"Very good, Sergei," said Ahmad as he put on a tight lipped smile and nodded with subdued pleasure.

As Bruslov concentrated on the bomb, he noticed that Majed lurking near-by watching his every move. Finally, Bruslov stopped, looked over at Majed, and asked,

"Do you know anything about nuclear weapons?"

"No. I was hoping to learn something about them by watching you. All my training has been with conventional explosives and C-4 plastics," said Majed.

Bruslov thought that this could be a cover story developed by Ahmad so Majed could stand around and report back if he thought something was suspicious with the reconfiguring work. What with the state of the bomb, Bruslov finally dismissed his misgivings about Majed and didn't pay any further attention to him. Based on his initial observations and gut feelings, Bruslov concluded that Omar and Majed were on the team to provide muscle and security for the mission.

After examining the bomb hulk for six hours, Bruslov announced that the stainless steel core of plutonium was operable. Little else was recognizable after being buried for years in salt water and mud. Every other component and instrument of the complex designed bomb apparatus had rusted to nothing but small stubs. Originally, the bomb was probably about ten feet in length. This bomb was designed for two sub critical pieces of material being placed inside the bomb casing. This atomic bomb structure is known as a gun-type method. His initial findings convinced him he could successfully produce a crude but still workable bomb. Bruslov recalled watching Soviet army training films of combat footage filed during the Afghanistan war that dealt with damaged atomic warheads. His present assignment wasn't that different from what he had studied.

The encased plutonium mass had been placed in the rear of the bomb. The arming trigger device, which was designed to be fired with a powerful charge of T.N.T. had been positioned in the nose. When dropped from a plane the T.N.T. trigger detonator would explode on contact with the ground. The arming device could also be programmed to set off the T.N.T. detonator before the bomb struck the ground.

This would yield an air-burst which delivered a powerful blast effect.

Faced with the poor condition of the bomb, Bruslov fashioned a rudimentary six foot sliding caged tube barrel from the stainless steel. Ultimately, the barrel would be sealed at both ends to compress the T.N.T. explosion toward the plutonium core. The important aspect of this engineering would be to insure that the detonator bullet was perfectly lined up to slam into the plutonium core with a force to cause the nuclear explosion. The plutonium core container had a positioning circle inscribed that told the bomb technician precisely where the arming triggering device was to be aimed.

After fashioning the sliding cage barrel rack for the detonator, Bruslov built a housing platform to secure the plutonium core in position to receive the detonator bullet precisely on the positioning circle. This engineering was not as complicated as the sliding cage tube rack but they both had to be in perfect alignment if the bomb was to have any chance of creating fission.

The final step for Bruslov was to develop a timing device that would fire the detonator at a preset time to allow the terrorists enough time to leave the blast area. Even if the bomb didn't produce the necessary energy to a nuclear explosion, the trigger explosion itself would create a dirty mess of dust, clouds and radioactive fall-out. Anyone near the explosion area wouldn't be safe from harm.

Bruslov noticed that Ahmad was becoming nervous about the time spent on the bomb reconfiguration. It was obvious that Ahmad was anxious to learn if the bomb could be made into a workable weapon. Bruslov knew that what he said would have a profound effect on the mission. Woven into his estimate was his own time table to execute his escape after the bomb was set to explode.

"I'm sure I can have the bomb ready for action in four, maybe five days," said Bruslov to a relieved Ahmad.

"I'm relying on your judgement. Let me know if you need new materials. Also, what is your best estimate of the reliability that this bomb will actually work?" asked Ahmad.

Bruslov refused to get trapped into guaranteeing a 100% reliability due to the condition and age of the plutonium core. "I am sure the arming detonator will work but after that I'd give it a 60-40 chance of reaching fissionable reaction and have the bomb go nuclear."

Ahmad walked over to a corner of the building and used his cell phone to call a secret telephone number belonging to an Islamic confidant in Washington, DC.

"Allah's message will be sent in five days," was left on the voice recorder. He felt sure that if American security agents were monitoring his cell phone transmissions they would not be able to decipher a meaning from the communication.

Armed with the additional ID numbers that Bruslov had discovered on the casing, Ahmad prepared a letter and mailed it to an Islamic Fundamentalist cleric living in New Jersey. The address was a letter drop that was used by Islamic cells throughout the US to communicate vital information to their commanders in London and Cairo. There was no need to write a long letter of explanation that, if intercepted by American security forces, could be traced back to the sender.

Secret coded numbers, known only to Ahmad, placed at the top of the letter were all that was necessary for the New Jersey cleric to know where to forward the message.

As the day dragged on Abdul approached his brother, "I'm tired from this work. I'm going home. I will leave the van and take my car."

Admad realized that his brother had done more than he had hoped was possible, "Yes, please accept my gratitude for your good work. Go home and rest. If I need you I'll contact you by phone. Go in peace my brother." Abdul sighed, left the building and walked to his car.

Abdul looked terrible and felt worse. Abdul lived in the historic village area of old Savannah in a furnished apartment. This area housed many old residences that were reminiscent of those that belonged to New England whaling ship owners and captains. Huge live oak trees lined the streets and were accompanied by beautiful planted bushes and tended shrubs that gave the area a garden atmosphere.

These were the same houses that had been occupied by northern civil war generals during the war of the unpleasantness.

After parking his car, Abdul opened his apartment door and walked into his world. He kicked off his shoes and fell into bed fully clothed and did not move for six hours. Finally, Abdul rose from his sleep, got out of his wrinkled clothes and showered for a long time in an effort to wake up. He dressed in clean fresh jeans and a dark T-shirt and drove slowly to Tubby's Tank House restaurant to eat some fresh seafood and drink strong black coffee. He tried to relax at his usual corner table. He hadn't seen Sherry for several days. As soon as he entered Tubby's, Sherry came to his table.

"You seem so preoccupied about something, Abdul."

"Oh, it's nothing. I'm just anxious about work and the antique shows that are coming up shortly." Abdul was attempting to engender a believable tone to his voice. How long, he said to himself, could he keep up this subterfuge?

"Could we have dinner some night soon, Sherry?" Abdul hoped that he could get her off her trend of questioning with a show of affection.

"Sure, we can work out something for dinner. That would be fine. Abdul, by the way, did you know the sailor you asked about was found dead last week?" Sherry's question was asked in her innocent manner that had always been her trademark. Upon hearing this question, Abdul felt the pricking sensation of needles on the back of his neck.

"Oh, I didn't know that. Was it in the papers?" said Abdul as his voice cracked.

"Well, the story has been in all the newspapers and on TV," said Sherry.

"His body was found about six blocks from here in an alley down near the waterfront." Sherry looked at Abdul and he just shook his head as if in disbelief. The more Sherry thought about it Abdul's behavior had seemed a lot different to her after Mike Hall was found dead. Hall's shrimp boat buddies had begun asking questions and spreading rumors about his death. One rumor, repeated endlessly, was that someone had killed Hall to put an end to his talking about the nuclear bomb ID plate. Mysteriously, the Savannah police reported they hadn't found the ID plate in Hall's apartment. The autopsy report stated that there were no traces of drugs found in Hall's blood. The early newspaper theory that speculated about a possible drug deal gone-bad as the motive for the homicide now looked weak.

As Abdul was finishing his meal, Sherry glanced his way several times and thought to herself, how could such an intelligent man be so ignorant about the death of a man she had identified for him? Was he playing dumb or didn't he care to discuss his past interest in Hall? Something didn't add up for Sherry but she couldn't put her finger on the problem. Her relationship with Abdul was becoming bizarre. Sherry began to feel she was subconsciously distancing herself from Abdul but really didn't know why it was happening.

As Abdul drank his black coffee, he stared into space. He realized he was never going to extract himself from his brother's plot against the US government. There could be no pretense in his mind any longer; he became filled with fear about saying no to any request from his brother.

Abdul left the restaurant and headed home. As he drove through traffic in a daze, he realized that he had reached his limit with Ahmad's mission to blackmail the US government. He never thought Ahmad would go this far to gain martyrdom in the Islamic Brotherhood. Now Abdul feared that his own life was in danger.

Just associating with the other two terrorists made him disgusted with himself. He had spent years in academia learning his chosen profession. Now, he was an errand boy for his younger brother, the Muslim terrorist.

He had leased a boat, building and rented a truck. All of these things were listed in his name and Savannah address. If an investigation came about he would be apprehended by the law authorities immediately. After that he would certainly be deported or perhaps sent to prison. As he saw himself sinking deeper into the plot he imagined his life drifting away to nothing. If he attempted to run away this afternoon an Islamic killer would undoubtedly be assigned to track him down and kill him without second thoughts. If this plot became compromised to the FBI they would arrest him and send him to prison. He was doomed in either event. His life was over no matter what happened. Abdul finally reached his apartment and laid down on his couch to think things over and attempt to resolve the conflict in his mind. Sleep and peace finally came.

As Abdul was leaving Tubby's, one of Sherry's girl friend work-mates asked,

"What's wrong with Abdul? He just left without saying good-bye."

Sherry shrugged her shoulders and said,

"I don't know the guy anymore. He's become a stranger."

Chapter VIII

Langley, Virginia

Captain Jack McQuesten, USN, sat at his desk in CIA headquarters reading the daily situation report (sitrep) he received about Islamic terrorist threats against US assets, foreign and domestic that seemed to be increasing daily. These daily summaries of FBI, National Security Agency, and Defense Department intelligence struck him as containing very little if anything really new.

He poured more coffee, checked the Wall Street Journal and looked through the Washington Times. He did this discretely, usually in private, as the division head didn't like the Times. It was felt that they were too fast and loose with classified information that fell into their hands. But it was amusing to read the latest political buzz that the Times featured. McQuesten surmised that his division boss didn't appreciate newspapers that had a conservative bent.

McQuesten's office staff was part of the National Resources, the US side of the clandestine services group. McQuesten's group tracked the activities of twenty-eight terrorist cells in the world, sponsored by Iran, Iraq, Libya, North Korea the PLO and Afghanistan or combinations of disaffected local groups.

The 1993 World Trade Center bombing in New York City and the Tokyo subway nerve gas attack, made it obvious even to casual observers that the western world was vulnerable to attack at any time by these groups, or others. Currently, the US government spends millions to train American military active duty and reserve units to respond to terrorist threats. Weapons of mass destruction (WMD) and their proliferation from the old Soviet Union stockpile used to be the big concern for the western security forces. In 1997 Russia openly admitted that the old Soviet Union had produced one hundred and thirty-two suitcase-sized weapons for use against the West. During the last inventory of these weapons, it was rumored that forty-eight were unaccounted for and presumed to be missing. Each suitcase weapon has the power of ten kilo tons of TNT.

It is well documented that ex-Russian KGB colonels openly roam the world consulting with terrorists groups and selling technology to the highest bidders.

One suitcase bomb used as a terror weapon could be ten times as powerful as the bomb that destroyed the Federal Office Building in Oklahoma City. Recent intelligence garnered by the US government proves that hundreds of off-shoot groups with terrorism on their minds and the means to carry out their threats must become our major concern.

McQuesten was born and raised in the Philadelphia suburbs. His father was a successful banker and his mother remained home to care for him and his younger brother and sister. During high school he played varsity football and was a member of the wrestling squad.

One day a school counselor approached McQuesten and said,

"Jack, the Navy offers an annual test for all high school seniors to see if they can qualify for an NROTC scholarship. This is a four-year scholarship at selected universities. I feel you should prepare yourself for this examination, which is scheduled in three weeks."

"Do you think I could pass it? I don't know anything about the Navy," said McQuesten as he let this information from his counselor soak into his mind.

"Yes, if you get your act together and think what it could mean to you. This could be a life changing opportunity," said the counselor.

"OK, I'll give it my best shot and burn some midnight oil over the books," said McQuesten. After serious preparation and study about the Navy, he passed the examination and qualified for an NROTC scholarship to Columbia University in New York City.

Upon graduation with a liberal arts degree and his Navy commission, he was ordered to sea duty aboard destroyers in Newport, RI. After four years of sea duty, he received surprise orders to the CIA. No sailor was ever happier to receive shore duty orders after bouncing around the Atlantic in the aging fleet of Navy destroyers. McQuesten's Vietnam CIA duty ended very abruptly with the fall of Saigon. He then qualified for naval aviation and spent the next six years flying fighter bombers off carriers in the Mediterranean Sea. When his eyes failed his flight physical, he returned to the surface fleet. He was promoted to skipper a destroyer escort and when he made commander he was ordered to command a new guided missile destroyer home ported in Newport. After that two-year tour he was promoted to Captain and received orders back to the CIA. Upon his second tour within the CIA they assigned his code name, Iron Hand.

Like many military officers who were stationed at the CIA, Iron Hand rented a large two bedroom apartment in McLean. He drove to work in his perfectly detailed XJ6 Jaguar taking a different route every day to throw off anyone who might be tracking his movements. When asked by any new acquaintance what he did for a living, he always answered in a matter of fact and bored manner, "I work in the Pentagon." This usually was enough to satisfy a normal person's meddling curiosity. Iron Hand thought that no one in their right mind would want to talk about the Pentagon.

Iron Hand's assistant was Sara Diamond. Sara was a fifteen-year veteran of the CIA and had extensive experience with the Directory of Analysis. She regularly reviewed, cataloged and correlated all the intelligence contact reports from anywhere that dealt with any threats against the CONUS. These reports were subsequently computerized and listed by their probability of being credible. Names, pictures and backgrounds of known terrorists were updated daily.

Dissemination was restricted to very few of Iron Hand's group. Diamond had twenty people reporting directly to her at the Langley headquarters.

Recently, Diamond had been receiving reports, some no more than overheard stories from paid informers in London pubs, that an Islamic Brotherhood attack might be in the initial planning stages against the US mainland. The target area in the US was thought to be along the US east coast. This thin information was sent to Iron Hand along with his morning top secret sitrep reports, that recapped any known or suspected foreign threats to the US. These bits of intelligence reminded Diamond of the pieces of the puzzle they failed to put together meaningfully prior to the 1993 World Trade Building attack.

"I always think how much money we pay for these reports and stories about threats to the US mainland. What good comes from worrying about a possible threat if we don't get some names and where the threat is coming from?" said Iron Hand to Diamond.

Sara Diamond looked over her shoulder and saw Iron Hand was reading his sitrep and not looking at her. She had a flippant remark ready to throw back at Iron Hand but she bit her lips. She was however, thinking to herself, "Oh, for heaven's sake, quit complaining and grumbling about the sources and the process. Just keep this information in the back of your mind. Perhaps it might come together down the road and we'll all be ahead of the power curve if any of this stuff ever turns out to be real."

Iron Hand, of course, would never knew what Diamond had been thinking or that she was probably correct in her assessment. It was difficult for anyone to deal with bits of information without the back-up of solid data, names and real intelligence. He felt there was a good probability the Islamic Brotherhood agents planted phony stories in known western listening posts to throw us off the real track. Iron Hand longed for a real contact on his radar screen, not just a fake return echo.

Sara Diamond and her sister grew up in a Navy family. Her father served as a line officer for twenty four years and retired with the rank of Captain. The family lived in Newport, RI during her high school years while her father completed two tours of sea duty on destroyers as the commanding officer. These tours were followed by more duty in Newport with welcome orders to the Naval War College.

She attended Rogers High School and spent many lonely days with her sister and mother, worrying about their father on his long deployments at sea. When her dad retired, the family settled in West Tisbury on Martha's Vineyard.

Upon graduating from Smith College, Sara went into government service at the State Department but found it too tame. Sara's retired father pulled a few strings to arrange CIA interviews and soon thereafter, she was able to transfer to The Company. Sara was a good solid nine. She was five foot eight, brunette with blue eyes and had cool slinky moves on the dance floor, which she regularly practiced in clubs around Georgetown and Alexandria. A few of her Company girl friends asked why she hadn't landed Iron Hand, but Sara replied, "Iron Hand's not my cup of tea; I like older guys but he's too set in his ways."

Sara's apartment was full of native stuff she had picked up during her early tours with the State Department in Africa and China. One tour in France had turned her into a total Francophile. She felt more at home on the Champs Elysees than walking along Pennsylvania Avenue in Washington, DC.

After weeks of scanning apparently useless bits of foreign intelligence about possible Islamic terror attacks against the US mainland, Iron Hand was deeply absorbed one morning with the Wall Street Journal, black coffee and his slumping tech stock portfolio. When he saw the blinking red light on his direct secure telephone line to the assistant Director's office. Iron Hand reached out, picked up the receiver,

"McQuesten here."

"Iron Hand, this is George Tilghman. Call right back on your secure line."

After several clicks and two or three seconds, Tilghman came on the line.

"Iron Hand, we have major league, big time trouble. The New York FBI office has received a Federal Express letter from an Islamic Brotherhood terrorist organization in London. They are demanding $5 billion in seven days or they are threatening to explode a nuclear bomb in a major populated area of the US mainland. Copies of the threat letter are being delivered to the President, Directors of the FBI and CIA, Secretary of Defense, and the NSA Director. There will be restricted distribution of the threat letter at this point in time to prevent any possible news leak and public panic. You will receive a copy of the threat letter from the

CIA Director within the hour. We are taking this threat very seriously. A meeting of the National Security Council is scheduled in two hours. I want you at this meeting and be prepared to answer questions about what your group has been doing. This will be a CIA responsibility since the FBI doesn't have the military hardware that will be needed to cope with these people when we get down to cases with this threat. Alert your top staff people that they can start the wheels turning."

The secure line went dead and Iron Hand replaced his receiver in the cradle. He took a deep breath and went to his window, looked out over the lawn and the the wooded Virginia countryside grounds that led out to the Potomac River. He thought to himself, those bastards have gone and done it this time. He returned to his desk and stared at the miniature American flag displayed on his desk. He kept it there at all times. He was proud to be fighting the enemies of America and glad the CIA had given him the responsibility of battling them. He exhaled heavily.

His next move was to have Diamond's staff bring all their files to his office that contained any report or reference they had collected concerning threats from any Islamic Brotherhood group. Names, faces and pictures of known terrorists could be critical to getting a handle of who was behind this threat. Without any formal authorization, Iron Hand gave Diamond the news about the threat and told her he was bending the rules by plugging her in to the loop.

"It would probably be smart to cancel any plans for the next ten days," said Iron Hand to Sara as she stared at Iron Hand. She had the sudden urge to light up a cigarette but she quit smoking three years ago.

"You and selected members of your staff will probably have to bunk at Langley for the duration of this emergency," said Iron Hand.

"What else can you tell me at this point?" said Sara.

Before Iron Hand had time to think further, the red light on his telephone was blinking again.

"McQuesten here."

He recognized the calm voice of George Tilghman but it was more tense.

"The Director has assigned the code words, "Blue Shield" for this operation. Any message traffic relating to this operation will only be routed to the President, Vice-President, Chairman of the Joint Chiefs, CIA, FBI and the NSA plus your team. Report immediately to the Director's alternate office in the Old Executive Office Building beside the White House. You are expected to have an initial game plan ready in six hours to present to the President and his national security advisors."

The secure line went dead. There was no time for cordial good-byes. Moments later a marine courier was standing at his desk with a mail packet marked urgent, "Blue Shield." Iron Hand signed off, acknowledging his receipt of the mail packet, and the marine left. Moments later, Iron Hand was reading the threat letter. There was little reason not to regard this threat seriously.

The letter mentioned two separate sets of nuclear bomb ID serial numbers that Iron Hand sensed were authentic and credible. Based upon his experience with tactical nuclear weapons and warheads, the numbers told him this was an Air Force weapon: not Army or Navy.

Iron Hand punched his inter-com,

"Sara, would you please come in here."

"Sara, this is an opportunity for you to shine. Take these MOS numbers and process them through the Joint Chiefs Staff nuclear weapons data bases. We need to determine what these numbers may mean. What are we looking at here? What type of weapon? What weight or size of warhead? What kind of Air Force plane would carry a weapon with these ID numbers? We also must try and figure out how these people got hold of the numbers and even, maybe the weapon itself."

"What is your gut feel about this threat?" asked Sara.

"I think this is the real deal," said Iron Hand.

Sara's blue eyes seemed to get larger when she heard Iron Hand say it was the real deal. She turned and walked briskly back to her office. The words, the real deal kept running through her mind: the real deal, the real deal.

Normally, Iron Hand would drive his Jaguar down the Washington Memorial Parkway, across the Teddy Roosevelt bridge near the Iwo Jima memorial, take a left to E Street, then over to seventeenth and through the West Executive avenue gates into the White House Compound. He had made the trip regularly since being assigned to duty with the CIA. But this time things would be different. He wanted time to think and not worry about driving through traffic.

He called for a sedan and driver to take him downtown for his secret meeting. He went in the seventeenth and Pennsylvania Avenue entrance to the Old Executive Office Building. Iron Hand walked through the crowed parking lot, up ten steps to the doors of the Old Executive Office building, across the black and white marble floor that had been installed after the Civil war. He did not wait for the elevator but took the stairs, two at a time, up to the fourth floor to the Director's office.

George Tilghman was waiting for him to get his initial reaction and assessments to the threat letter. Before walking over to the White House Tilghman told Iron Hand to sit down for a few minutes to go over his notes.

"These White House political wonks will do anything to protect the Administration by putting their spin on this emergency. Sometimes these guys come across as major league ass-holes. I'll handle all of their questions and if they jump on you, I'll come to your rescue. Try and keep your answers to only what you know. Stay away from conjecture and anything political. If they start to get tough just relax and roll with the punches. If I need your help, I'll nod to cue you in. Don't give them anything that they can throw back at us later." Iron Hand nodded.

Iron Hand mused, "Frankly, I never liked these White House guys. I'd like to punch-out the lights of those little candy-asses."

Tilghman looked at Iron Hand with a smile. Iron Hand thought to himself, "Is this guy reading my mind. No wonder he has this big job."

After Tilghman and Iron Hand completed the dry-run meeting in the Old Executive Office Building, they left and walked briskly across the driveway to a room in the lower level of the White House. Tilghman was seated at the head of a long table in the subdued secret Situation Room. This room was chosen because there would be no opportunity for conversation vibrations to bounce off windows that could possibly be picked up by spies using sophisticated microphones. Several maps that detailed the eastern US coastline were hung on the walls behind Tilghman. The walls not used for maps were draped with heavy curtains from the ceiling to the floor. It was announced that the meeting would be taped and transcripts would be available to everyone cleared for this operation, "Blue Shield." Iron Hand was sitting at the right of Tilghman.

Tilghman began the meeting with an opening statement that summed up the US position and a range of possible responses to the threat letter. The government could do nothing and call the bluff of the terrorists; Unleash our assets and come down hard on any organization that looked like they had ties to these terrorists; Signal that we were prepared to meet their demands and buy time to track them down; Or, adopt any combination of the above of other ideas. Men from the other security agencies sat with rapt attention to every word. Iron Hand sensed that several of the agency people were ready to pounce on any opening to state that their agency could have done a better job predicting this threat was imminent.

Iron Hand asked himself, "Is this the time to display old inter-service rivalry?" Anyone who ever worked at the senior staff level in the Pentagon knew that inter-service, agency and departmental rivalry was on-going and prolific. No opportunity to kick the others guy's butt was ever over looked. This wouldn't be some overt act but just a subtle little comment that pricked the target with the message, "We could have done it better."

Pete Buckley of the FBI asked Tilghman,

"What information do we have in our files about these London Islamic Brotherhood guys who sent the threat letter?" Tilghman turned to Iron Hand and cued him to answer the question.

"We currently know little about the men who are in this London based terrorist organization. Admittedly our files are thin about this specific group. We have had little or no intelligence about them. However, we have received signals in the last ninety days that a terrorist plot against the US mainland was in the works. Generally, we sift through these reports and attempt to tie them in with other intelligence picked up through our embassy listening posts throughout Europe. We are tracking over two dozen terrorist groups that are state sponsored or renegade groups funded by international criminal organizations."

Buckley seemed satisfied with what he heard. Thilghman gave Iron Hand a nod that meant, "well done." Iron Hand thought he had said enough. Basically, he knew the government didn't know about these guys.

Buckley raised his hand again to signal he wanted another crack at Iron Hand.

"Do you have informants on the ground or inside any of these Islamic organizations that feed us intelligence that has proven reliable in the past?"

Iron Hand started to answer but Tilghman cut him off and jumped in. "We don't admit openly about our informants from the inside of any terrorist organizations. All our information is considered semi-reliable but subject to review and confirmation from second or third sources. This threat was not foreseen by any of the US security apparatus, foreign or domestic."

When sharks smell blood in the water they circle their prey and strike rapidly. Iron Hand sensed he was the prey and began looking around the table to see which guys were the sharks. Larry Paine, a domestic policy wonk and Presidential political advisor, asked Tilghman, "If we have moles in some of the terrorist groups around Europe, why is it that I'm just learning about it now, after the threat letter has been received demanding $5 billion. The Administration will come off looking like we don't know what's going on."

Tilghman looked Paine dead in the eyes and said,

"We work in a secret world and many of our contacts are known only to a few people in Washington. We consider their information reliable only when we can reconfirm it with corroborative evidence. When we obtain this evidence we pass this intelligence on to the President. If we don't obtain some confirmation we file it as unsubstantiated. We will never be caught passing along rumors to the Administration that may turn out to be wrong and prove embarrassing."

Paine seemed to back off and appeared to be making mental notes and signaled he was through asking questions.

Iron Hand thought to himself, enough finger pointing and name-calling. Let's get down to business. Tilghman picked up the ball and re-summarized the meeting. All the other security agency representatives had come to listen and weren't ready to add a great deal of original thought. They quickly agreed with Tilghman about adopting a speedy course of action to resolve this threat to the US mainland. Everyone enthusiastically pledged their respective agency's cooperation.

Tilghman said, "I'm going to give the floor to Captain McQuesten for some time so he can relate to you what his CIA group has come-up with. After listening to his remarks we will then open the meeting up to your thoughts and commentary."

Iron Hand began his remarks by stating he thought the bomb threat in the letter was genuine and not a cover story to ensure that the US paid the $5 billion in blackmail. Iron Hand felt there was a high probability that the terrorists would attempt to detonate the bomb whether the US paid the ransom or not.

"If the government chooses to pay the ransom, the bankers who received the money might not be able to communicate that the blackmail had been paid, thereby satisfying one of the major demands of the letter. We must not assume that by paying the blackmail the bomb will not be turned against us." Iron Hand then concluded, "The government was faced with a distinct possibility that even after the ransom was paid, the bomb threat must still be treated as ongoing and real. Any separate cell of terrorists operating alone and in possession of a recovered nuclear bomb, probably would have not have any motivation to surrender the bomb anyway. They could use the weapon to blackmail us again or use it against other countries."

The meeting adjourned concluding that the threat was real, that time was running very short, and that the terrorists were probably prepared to detonate the bomb even if the US paid their ransom demands. All agreed that Iron Hand was the right man to lead the task force of Operation Blue Shield. The room cleared out except for Tilghman and Iron Hand. Tilghman started talking,

"If this threat letter turns out to be real and we don't stop them, the President and his party will be dead politically for ages. This is why we are giving you broad personal authority for this operation. Due to the gravity of this threat and the short time frame, Captain, we are going to give authority to take many matters into your own hands without checking back here for authorizations. Keep us informed about all your moves. Work with your office staff and we'll get plugged in through them. Just remember to classify all message traffic "Blue Shield."

Back at Langley in Iron Hand's office, Sara had gone to work immediately. She had dated a computer jockey at the Joint Chiefs Service nuclear weapon data base service center. She had dated him several times but dusted him before the relationship got too serious.

"Hello Brad, Sara here. I've got a favor to ask of you. Top Secret, of course. We must have some immediate answers. What can you do for me, honey?"

She could almost hear Brad panting over the telephone. This call for help from Sara was more than he had ever dared to dream.

"Listen, baby, if there is something in these computers you want, just tell me. We will move heaven and earth. How much time do I have for this project?"

"We need this yesterday."

In ten hours Sara and the Joint Chief Service center had pieced together a sketchy story of a 1958 mid air collision between a B-47 bomber and an F-86 fighter interceptor over Savannah, Ga. during a routine training mission.

Apparently, the collision resulted in the bomber dropping an unarmed nuclear weapon into Wassaw Sound off Tybee Island beach before risking a crash landing at Hunter Army airfield in Savannah. After ten days of searching in the shallow waters off Tybee Island, the Air Force declared the nuclear warhead bomb component could not be found and listed it as irretrievable. The old report contained several AEC nuclear weapon serial numbers on the bomb that was jettisoned from the Air Force bomber.

Sara's department went to work with the computer history and after two hours of analysis confirmed that the numbers in the threat letter matched several of the numbers from the lost bomb dropped off Tybee Island, near Savannah, Georgia.

Sara buzzed Iron Hand's office and said, "We believe we have matched the numbers in the Islamic threat letter. I'm on my way to show you the data."

"Those Islamic bastards have the correct numbers off the atomic bomb, or maybe, they have even recovered the old Air Force bomb and the mass of radioactive U-235. This is the weapons grade material that every terrorist in the world wants to have. They will attempt to reconfigure the warhead and make a crude dirty bomb to blow up part of Savannah. My assessment is they could target anywhere as far north as Charleston and down the coast south to Jacksonville. The highest probability target area is Savannah, Ga. I'm guessing the terrorists would not risk transporting their bomb too far from where it was found," surmised Iron Hand after listening to Sara's research and input from staff members.

"Sara, get these tentative conclusions to Tilghman, ASAP. Tell him I'm leaving shortly for Savannah to establish a Command Post at Hunter Army Airfield to begin our search efforts. Ask Tilghman to authorize a CIA plane to take me to Savannah. I'll want to leave in approximately two hours. Also, tell him I'm recommending we sortie our big naval assets from NAS Jacksonville immediately but not too fast so as to attract media attention that something big is up.

Iron Hand picked up the secure line and asked that the CIA Gulf Stream jet at Reagan Washington National airport stand by for immediate departure to Savannah's Hunter Army Airfield. ETA Savannah, Ga. after lift off would be in three hours. Confirmation came back that the authorization from Tilghman had indeed come through moments before.

Iron Hand sat at his desk and for a moment thinking: Do I know anyone in the Savannah area who knows the town and can get me around without stirring up the general public. Then the answer hit him: His squadron buddy and wingman on his last Mediterranean cruise aboard the carrier USS Kennedy, Lt. Deane Paulson, code name handle, GameBird.

It was perfect; Paulson had retired from the Navy with full pension after a second flight accident that left him unable to pass the flight physical. He returned to his native Savannah to take over the family's marine yacht brokerage business.

Iron Hand picked up his phone and asked his secretary,

"Lory, see if you can find the telephone number of a Deane Paulson, in the Savannah, Georgia area. If you can find it, get him on the line. Don't let on about anything. Just tell him I need to talk to him right away."

Lory had never heard of Paulson and she wondered if this was important to the mission or just another slow walk down memory lane that Iron Hand was taking to relax. Six minutes later Lory buzzed Iron Hand's inter office speaker phone;

"I have a Mr. Paulson on line three. Apparently he remembers you well, but doesn't understand why there is an urgent call from you."

Iron Hand picked up his telephone and punched the blinking light,

"Hello GameBird. This is Jack McQuesten. How the hell are you? How long has it been?" Iron Hand was putting on his warm good old boy voice to smooth things out.

Paulson replied,

"Everything is fine down here. We spend most of our time staying cool, swatting mosquitoes and cheering for the Sand Gnats." Paulson's voice trailed off and it was clear he was wondering what this call was all about after so many years.

"Listen, Deane, I'm on my way to Savannah on official Navy business. I may need you to help me with a few details around town. Introductions to the right people without causing any excitement about me. This is National Security stuff. I have to play this low key as long as possible. You remember: Go do your job yesterday, come back the day before. Can you spare me some time later today and maybe part of next week? I may need some local skids greased. This might turn out to be important. What do you say; are you still a GameBird?"

"McQuesten, I mean Captain, you have never sounded so serious. Just tell me when and where to meet you in Savannah. I certainly never expected to receive a call like this but it must be important so there will be no joking around."

Iron Hand accepted the offer of help and said, "Deane, meet me at Hunter Army Airfield in three hours. We'll have dinner tonight and I'll fill in the details. See you soon."

Iron Hand left the old Executive Office building and headed directly to the Reagan National airport and the small terminal for private planes. The Gulf Stream was turning over its powerful engines. A small bag he always kept packed was fetched for him from home and was already stowed aboard. His team was aboard too. He settled down in the director's chair, buckled up, took a sip of coke offered him by the Navy steward and picked up the secure phone beside his chair.

"Sara, You'll have to be on office duty 24/7 to coordinate all the details from your end. I'll be depending on you. Call the Marines at Parris Island to have one Rifle Company placed on full alert for a possible airlift to the Savannah waterfront or the Tybee Island area. I don't know if we will need that much muscle but I'd rather be over-loaded than coming up short at the last minute. Also, call the

Marine air station in Beaufort to put six F-18's on stand-by alert status. I want three F-18's on run-way alert for air cover over Savannah at my direction and Operation Blue Shield. The weapons release code words will be Blue Light. Got all that? It might be nice to have a little jet thunder rolling around the skies over Savannah if our terrorists are busy plotting our destruction."

"Yes, sir."

"OK. Get on this right away. I'll get back to you shortly after I get to Savannah."

Iron Hand leaned back on the headrest and, while thinking about the mission, the dinner with his old wingman Paulson, and chatter about old times, drifted off to sleep as the Gulf Stream jet lifted off the airport runway and climbed to its 35,000 feet cruising altitude.

Chapter IX

Savannah, Georgia

The Gulf Stream jet landed at Hunter Airfield at 2:45pm. Two CIA Special Operations agents met the plane and briefed Iron Hand on their progress to set up his Hunter AAF command post. Ultra secure communication frequencies and back-up channels were established to protect all his messages to Langley where Sara was routing Operation Blue Shield traffic to the National Security Counsel.

After approving the preparation work for his command post, Iron Hand was ready to meet his old wingman Paulson. He was anxious to see how difficult it was going to be to run the secret operation in Savannah without alerting the media. The last thing Iron Hand wanted was a bunch of news hounds snooping around trying to get the scoop on Operation Blue Shield.

Paulson sat in the waiting room reserved for civilians and minor dignitaries. Iron Hand walked through the door, "Deane-san. Thank you for coming here. How's everything going with you?" Paulson jumped up and extended his hand,

"How do you do, Captain McQuesten. Man, do you look good. Have you been working out, or what?"

"Well, the Navy brass keeps me on my toes," said Iron Hand.

"What are you flying these days?" asked Paulson with a smile on his face.

"The only thing I fly is a desk in the Pentagon. Deane, I still remember your last landing on the Kennedy," said Iron Hand.

"My landing gear gave out after I missed the #1 wire and I slid across the flight deck. Luckily I caught the #3 wire, or they'd still be looking for me," said Paulson.

"Yeah, back then we were bullet-proof, or so we thought. Those were the days, flying A4D's for the VA-153 Blue Tails Flies squadron," said Iron Hand as they both laughed.

"We need to go where we can talk privately," said Iron Hand, as he wanted to get down to business. "I've got a little office set-up right here at Hunter. Let's head over there," said Iron Hand. They got into a sedan and drove about one mile to Iron Hand's Command Post.

Iron Hand adhered to the CIA policy of divulging just enough information to get a job done, strictly on a need to know basis. "Here's why I came to Savannah, Deane. The government has learned that there are some well financed bad-guys around here that are running a big drug operation. I've been ordered to find out if this is true or just some bad intelligence. Have you, or any of your friends, seen any new faces that may be operating large boats around Tybee Island? They may have even rented a substantial residence to run their operation. They might even be using a cover story about salvaging sunken ships, that sort of thing, to cover their real intentions."

Paulson let the information from Iron Hand sink into his mind. He thought for a moment before saying, "Well, I'm not on the cutting edge of that line of activity. Sounds more like a question for the local police, not me."

"Washington doesn't want to get the local police involved just yet. This may turn out to be a bad piece of intelligence. They don't want a lot of law enforcement agencies looking into this right now," said Iron Hand.

"Nothing comes to my mind off hand. Let me think about this over dinner. I do know a few guys in the marine salvage business. I could ask them about it; if they have noticed any unusual activity around Tybee," said Paulson.

"Now you're talking," said Iron Hand as he gave Paulson a thumbs-up.

"Incidentally, Deane, what I have told you is confidential. If anything develops I'll try to keep you plugged in and up to date."

"I understand. My lips are sealed."

Paulson looked at his old buddy McQuesten and said, "You look like you could use a cold beer. I know a restaurant on East River Road by the Wilmington River. This place will give you a good feeling of Tybee Island, Wassaw Sound and the local waterfront. It's about a mile from my business. They serve fresh shrimp that they buy right off the boats."

"Let's go find that restaurant," said Iron Hand. They left Iron Hand's office and climbed into Paulson's new company pick-up truck and drove off. Two FBI agents followed along discreetly at a prudent distance in a dark maroon sedan. Iron Hand had his CIA cell phone/pager tuned to a special single side-band frequency so he could easily communicate with them. His little electronic gizmo was designed to look like a chrome plated ball-point pen in his breast pocket.

"As Paulson drove through traffic he began wondering about the smugglers that McQuesten was looking for. "Can

103

you tell me a little more about these drug dudes you're after?"

Iron Hand realized that Paulson was buying into his cover story about drug dealers. He didn't feel good about stringing his old buddy along but he had to keep up the cover story. If something leaked out differently it might be disastrous.

"Just that they are probably not US citizens. Maybe from the middle-east or Hispanic guys that are very dangerous," said Iron Hand as he purposely shortened up his modest soliloquy about the bad guys he wanted to find.

Paulson tightened up his lips and shook his head from side-to-side. He drove on without any other comment. Paulson realized this could turn into something dangerous. This was not just some casual retired navy jet jockey reunion.

Paulson pulled into Tubby's Tank House restaurant driveway and they walked inside amid the early dinner crowd and a few hangers-on at the bar drinking beer.

Paulson whispered to Iron Hand, "If anyone asks what we're doing here, I'll tell them you're looking at one of the boats I've got for sale."

"Sound OK to me," said Iron Hand.

They got themselves seated at a table with their backs to the wall that gave them a good view of the bar and semi-privacy to talk.

"Who's the big blonde coming our way?" asked Iron Hand.

"That's Sherry. She more or less runs the bar area and handles all the drink orders for the dinner crowd. Every guy in this part of town has taken his best shot at her and struck out, as far as I know. I think she's dating an Arab or Pakistani guy who works with antiques and ancient art works. She's divorced with one kid. That's all I know."

"What can I get you guys from the bar?' said Sherry as she sized up Iron Hand.

"How about a cold beer. What have you got?" said Paulson.

"Oh, chocolate, strawberry and vanilla. All the usual flavors," said Sherry.

Iron Hand thought, cute and a sense of humor too. I like that. They finally ordered Miller Lite drafts which came right away. Paulson began reflecting about a shrimp boat crewman who had been killed ten days ago and that his murder remained unsolved. It was known in the waterfront bars that the dead crewman was a regular drinker at Tubby's Tank House. It wasn't unusual for the shrimp boat crewmen to drink up most of their wages after their boats tied up at the pier. This unsolved murder was the only event Paulson could think of that was more or less different from the daily routine activity on the waterfront.

"For starters, we might ask Sherry if she has heard any news about the sailor that was found dead not too far from here. These shrimp boat crewmen and Captains might have some of the information that you're looking for," said Paulson with a look that said, at least I'm trying to come up with an idea.

"OK," said Iron Hand. "When she comes back, ask her that question. We'll see what happens." Iron Hand took a long pull on his beer and watched to see how Paulson handled the question with Sherry. Iron Hand didn't understand how questions about an unsolved murder was going to help his investigation.

At this point however, he had nothing else to go on. When she came back, Paulson waited for the right moment and said,

"Sherry, I was telling my friend about the shrimp boat crewman who was found murdered. Did anyone ever come-up with any theories about his murder?"

"You mean Mike Hall?" Sherry asked with a funny look on her face.

"Yeah, I think that was his name," said Paulson.

Sherry looked around the bar and said, "His buddies from Miss Thunderbolt are sitting right over there. Maybe they'll tell you what happened."

"Would they talk to us?" asked Paulson.

"Are you kidding. Buy them some beer and they'll talk your ear off. Ask them any questions you have," said Sherry.

"OK, I'm up to the challenge. Send them a round of what ever they're drinking. Tell them we have a few questions about their dead buddy, Hall," said Paulson.

Sherry looked at Paulson and said, "Before we get to that, how about introducing your friend here." Iron Hand stood up and looked directly at Sherry and said,

Please excuse me for being rude, my name is McQuesten, Jack McQuesten. Iron Hand extended his hand and Sherry engaged it with a warm firm grasp.

"Nice to meet you, Jack."

A couple of minutes passed. One of the crewmen came over to Paulson and Iron Hand's table. "Thanks for the beer. What do you want to know about Hall? I worked with him on Miss Thunderbolt."

"Nothing special about our interest. We were just wondering, why do you think he was murdered?" ask Paulson.

"I'll tell you the quick and dirty thoughts that are going around about Hall's death. Mike was an OK guy, not too smart, but he was never in any trouble with the cops. He didn't do drugs but he drank a lot of beer, most of the time right here in Tubby's. The only thing we know is he found an odd piece of brass metal in a shrimp net that had military markings or ID code numbers. He showed it off for a few nights and took it home to polish it up. He figured he could sell it and make some money. Then one night, he gets bumped off. All of us have been talking about this since it happened, but the cops haven't done anything. It's turned into a dead issue. You're the first people who have asked about him in weeks. Are you guys private eye's, or something? You don't look like the cops."

"Was all of this that you're telling us in the papers?" asked Iron Hand whose interest in the death of Hall suddenly had some relevance to his mission. My god thought Iron Hand, perhaps Paulson has stumbled on to something that's going to be important.

"No. None of the stuff about the brass metal ID plate ever made the papers, as far as I know," said the crewman. "Hey guys, I have to get back to my buddies. Thanks for the beer."

"Deane, it was a stroke of genius to bring me here. I just got lucky and learned something that ties-in with some intelligence we have back in Washington," said Iron Hand.

He settled back in his chair for a moment, letting the crewman's story sink into his mind.

Sherry came by the table to check for another beer order. "Can I get you guys another round? Or, are you ready to order some food?"

"We're ready for some fresh shrimp, Sherry. By the way, what was the name of the boat Hall worked on? Did you say, Miss Thunderbolt?" asked Paulson.

"Yep. That's the boat. Captain Rogers owns it. It's always tied up at the pier across the road," said Sherry.

"If you don't mind us asking one more thing, did you ever see Hall passing around the piece of metal ID plate his buddy just told us about? asked Iron Hand.

"Oh sure, that first night, everyone in the bar was looking at it," said Sherry.

As Iron Hand sat eating his dinner, all he could think about between bites was interviewing the skipper of Miss Thunderbolt. Also, since he was dealing with an Islamic Fundamentalist terror group, this dark skinned Arab or Pakistani man that Sherry dated aroused some interest. He was getting some subtle vibes in his mind to check out this guy. He didn't want to get Sherry excited about talking too much with strangers. He wondered about how to get information from her and not cause her to tell the boy friend some men were asking questions about him.

Iron Hand always thought he was pretty good at getting women to do what he wanted. This would test his resolve about how clever he was. His cover story about investigating a big local drug ring might not hold up with Sherry.

Iron Hand and Paulson finished eating and used the excuse of needing to stretch their legs to cross the road to check-out the moored shrimp boats. A shrimp boat isn't a thing of beauty. They are working boats and wouldn't win a contest for spit and polish. Most of the boats tied up looked like they had just returned from a war zone. Captain Van, Star One, Dragonard, Amanda Lynn, Treasure and finally, Miss Thunderbolt, all nested together looking like a mothballed fleet of WW II mine sweepers.

"I've seen enough here for now, Deane. I want to interview the skipper of Miss Thunderbolt to see if I can learn more about the murdered crewman. Maybe he can point us in another direction. We will need a complete list of this man's buddies and obtain statements from them. What they know or think they know about the crime. This would be a good job for the local FBI field agents."

Iron Hand said to himself: "I need to check out the guy Sherry is dating; the Arab or Pakistani guy. Where does he live? What is his name? What does he do for a living? Check for all that kind of information. This is another job for the FBI."

Paulson was sitting in his pick-up writing notes to himself about what his next job was to help McQuesten. He also volunteered that he would ask around the yacht brokering firms to see if they had rented any boats for salvage operations in Wassaw Sound.

"Jack, why not ask your FBI agent buddies to check with the Coast Guard station to see if they boarded or inspected any vessels in Wassaw Sound recently that are involved in salvage or diving work. This would be a good job for them to get some straight answers from the Coast Guard," Paulson said, with a proud look on his face. He seemed to be getting into the spirit of things.

"Great idea, Deane," said Iron Hand.

"Since I'm already here, I think I will go back and talk to the barmaid, Sherry. I've got a feeling she knows more than she's letting-on," said Iron Hand.

"Yeah, I'll bet you're right, Paulson chimed in, but you don't want to scare her into to claming up."

"Or go running to her boyfriend and tell him some strangers were asking about him. The only trouble is, I'm working with a short time frame and there isn't a lot of time to waste on formalities," said Iron Hand as he sat in the pick up truck thinking for a moment about his next move.

"Deane-san, you've had a big day. Why don't you head home and let me take it from here. You have my number at Hunter if you come up with anything. Call anytime and someone will be there. They'll find me if I don't answer the phone myself." With this Paulson said good night and headed home. Iron Hand stood in Tubby's parking lot and watched Paulson's pick up truck taillights disappear down East River Road. As Iron Hand turned to head back into Tubby's, he pulled out his special cell phone/pager and ordered the FBI agents to stand by and stake out Tubby's.

Once inside the restaurant he headed back to his table. Sherry spotted Iron Hand as he came through the door. Their eyes met and held for about ten seconds. Iron Hand felt some chemistry and thought that Sherry had the same feeling. Iron Hand sensed that Sherry was putting out her welcome mat.

Sherry walked over to his table and said, "I'm glad you came back. I didn't think I would see you again this evening. What can I do for you?"

Iron Hand looked straight into Sherry's eyes and said, "What time do you get off work? I hope you don't mind my being so direct."

"No problem with your approach but it would be nice if I knew more about you."

"Sorry about that. I haven't been very good about telling you about myself," said McQuesten. "My buddy has gone home and I was hoping that we could talk," said McQuesten as he ducked her question to learn more about him.

Sherry looked a little weak in the face, and said, "Actually, I'm off work now. Do you want to go down the road a little way and get a drink? If you're not driving, we can go in my car."

Iron Hand couldn't believe how fast things were moving along. To think he was in Washington eight hours ago not knowing where the day would take him when he started.

"I'm in your hands, Sherry. I'm ready to leave if you are." Iron Hand picked up a packet of matches with Tubby's address and telephone. He slipped the matches into his pant pocket. They left together by the front door and climbed into Sherry's 1993 Olds rag top convertible. Iron Hand thought he smelled old French fries and hamburgers from Burger King in the back seat. He would never have a smell like that in his XJ6. He noticed the FBI agents pulling out of the parking lot as Sherry drove down East River Road a restaurant named The River's End. Iron Hand could only imagine what the two agents were saying to themselves about this little move he was putting on Sherry.

They were seated in the back of the Rivers End bar and Sherry started talking with a nice smile,

"Well Jack, are you down here looking for love in all the wrong places?"

Iron Hand smiled and didn't answer the question. He decided to play into the story the crewman had told him earlier.

"Sherry, I'm trying to learn more about Hall's murder and how it might tie-in with some drug smugglers we have been investigating. I'm interested in anything you can tell me about him or his friends. Anyone who you heard talking about him whether it's just rumors or stuff you observed in Tubby's. Sorry to hit on you with so much of this before we have really become acquainted," Iron Hand stopped and hoped he hadn't gone too far.

"Like I said before, Jack, what is your gig anyway? Are you a cop or some kind private eye working this murder case? I guess I don't understand why you're so interested in the Hall murder case," said Sherry with a puzzled look directed at Iron Hand.

"Perhaps I've been moving too quickly, Sherry. His buddy said that Hall had a piece of brass ID metal plate with some military code numbers. I guess that's what I'm mostly interested in at this point. Anything you can tell me about who has been interested in him or the brass ID metal plate would be a big help. Iron Hand decided to clam up because he knew he was moving way too fast with Sherry. Hopefully, Sherry would tell him something he didn't already know.

"Well, I don't know if I should say this or not, but a guy I have been seeing did ask me to point out Hall just days before he was found dead in an alley. No one knows about this except me. The cops never came around Tubby's so I didn't say anything. Actually, my friend's been acting so strangely of late I really don't have a lot of positive feelings about him." Sherry sat quietly looking contrite as she stared into her drink. "Am I doing a dumb thing by talking to you about this?"

"Sherry, I can assure you that you are doing the right thing. Don't worry about what someone is going to say because we talked. Please tell me about the man you are seeing and why you think he asked you to point out Hall," said McQuesten who waited, hoping for a good answer.

"The man I'm dating is named Adbul Rahman. He's an Egyptian from Cairo University working in Savannah for local libraries on middle-eastern culture and antiquities. He's in the US on a teaching visa and must leave in six months unless he gets an extension from the INS." Sherry sat for a moment and took a long sip of her drink and looked at Iron Hand for a reaction. Iron Hand gave her a look that said, yes, go on, you're doing great, don't stop now, it's getting good.

Sherry continued, saying that she told Abdul about the story of Hall and the brass ID plate the first day he was in Tubby's talking about it with his drinking buddies. She hadn't thought anything about it again until Abdul came to Tubby's and asked her to point out Hall. Two days later Hall was found dead.

"Do you think there is a connection between my pointing out Hall and his death?" Sherry asked in a voice that was pleading, please, say it isn't so. She was starting to feel ashamed of herself for giving up so much information about the man she was seeing regularly. Iron Hand feared he had pushed the conversation too far and in a low voice said,

"Sherry, you probably didn't do anything wrong, but I'm afraid I have to ask you, where does Abdul live?"

Sherry gave Iron Hand the address of Abdul's apartment in the Savannah historic district. After this, She became somewhat reticent and asked Iron Hand,

"Jack, maybe I have been talking too much about this?"

"No. Don't worry about it. Please go home now and don't mention to anyone that we talked. If Abdul is somehow mixed up in the death of Hall you might also be in danger. If we see each other again in Tubby's, don't pay attention to me unless I ask you to come to my table."

Sherry took a deep breath and looked straight into Iron Hand's eyes and said,

"I've always liked mysterious guys with a military, take charge attitude. But not the immature, gung-ho type. I tried that once. Now I'm divorced with a kid. I don't pop my cork for every guy who walks into Tubby's. I like your style, Jack, but I'm not desperate. You should know this now, up front." Sherry lowered her glance and waited for Iron Hand to react.

He spoke quietly,

"I like a woman who knows what she wants and has the courage to be up front about it. No waiting around, waiting for a guy to make the first move. We'll learn more about each other as I try to piece together this puzzle. If you know anything else give it to me now. There probably isn't too much time left for guess work."

Sherry was putting together her things and getting ready to leave when she said,

"Abdul told me to plan a trip to Disney World in a few days. He said he'd pay for everything travel expenses, food, lodging, the works. Would that be important for you to know?"

Iron Hand tried not to show any reaction in his face to this last little tidbit of information. He realized that this meant there was a short time-table for the terrorist operation and Abdul was attempting to warn his mistress to get away from ground zero. Iron Hand looked at Sherry and said,

"Well, it could be important. I will have to think about how it ties in with what we know." Iron Hand thought, no sense scaring to death the only good lead he had. Sherry climbed to her convertible and drove off into the night. Iron Hand had positive vibes that he was going to know her a lot better.

Chapter X

Savannah, Ga.

After getting back to Hunter Army Airfield, Iron Hand walked through the sparse BOQ hallway, entered his room, shed his clothes and fell into the king sized bed that was the only redeeming part of his quarters. Five hours later he awoke with his mind racing.

Iron Hand had given Abdul's address to the FBI and ordered them to set-up a round-the-clock stake out of the apartment. In addition, the FBI filed a request in a Washington, DC Federal court that remained open 24/7 to grant emergency orders for investigations involving national security. Permission was received to install a wire tap device on Abdul's telephone line, and also investigate his old telephone records, computer and banking records.

The FBI wouldn't have a problem bugging a telephone line since this was and old-hat trick. They were masters at tapping telephone lines of organized crime mobsters or white collar crime figures. Getting secret cooperation from a phone company was another matter, since it usually meant involving individuals with no security clearance and they could discover something about Operation Blue Shield. A leak or comment to the media by a careless telephone employee might bring in snooping news reporters looking for a big story.

By 6:00 A.M. the listening tap was installed and then the waiting game began. A team of FBI agents, parked near the apartment, posing as telephone repairmen, were ready for action. Federal authority was also obtained to install a cookie inside Abdul's computer to trace his traffic, review his stored memory and hard drive data. The installation of a cookie was easily accomplished through his Internet Service Provider (ISR). Any use of the telephone or computer by Abdul would be detected and recorded. The listening FBI agents would notify Iron Hand immediately at his Hunter Command Post.

Iron Hand spent the early morning in his humble BOQ quarters at Hunter collecting his thoughts and planning his next move. He soon felt the hot humid weather that was the trademark of the Savannah, Georgia low-country. He showered, shaved and put on fresh white skivvies to relax before heading over to his command post to check in with Langley. The window box AC was working hard to pump in cool air as the heat of the day began to climb. The old drab military curtains kept out some sun rays and heat but the room was becoming muggy.

Back at Langley, Sara walked down the undecorated hallway after a visit to the ladies room. The halls had closed doors with only room numbers and no names that might yield a hint who worked there or what went on behind the doors. She had spent the previous four days tracking the progress of Operation Blue Shield.

While eating lunch with her Company girl friend, Julie, they talked about their love life, and lack there of, and boy friends . This was a good break from the strain of Company business.

Julie was always interested in Sara's latest excuse for not landing Iron Hand. Julie pressed Sara on the subject on by asking,

"What's the matter with you? If McQuesten pulls off Operation Blue Shield successfully, he'll be a huge hero around here and quite the catch. I know lots of others who are sick with jealousy of you working so closely with him."

Julie had said, "Don't hand me that old line that he's too set in his ways. You can train him after you get a ring on your finger."

Sara thought, "Maybe Julie is right. Perhaps I have been too hasty about writing off McQuesten as a bad risk. It would be fun to do the cocktail party and dinner circuit with him in tow. It would also be great to make the other gals jealous." Sara began to think, "What was he doing right now? Why didn't he call to get the scoop from her?" Sara mused further that she had always liked older men. After all, the young guys didn't know how to treat a lady.

After eating a breakfast consisting of scrambled eggs, toast, orange juice and black coffee Iron Hand seemed ready to take on the morning with renewed vigor. He settled into his make shift Command Post and telephoned Langley on a secret frequency.

"Hello Sara, good to hear your voice again. I've decided the terrorist target is almost certainly Savannah. I have ninety percent of all our containment efforts focused here. We'll still have some good surveillance devoted to Charleston and Jacksonville but at reduced levels," he said.

"Here's our plan for detection around Savannah. Please polish this up and send it along to Tilghman and the others on the need to know list. Our FBI units are already searching the Savannah waterfront docks and cargo areas with unmarked vans that are packed with electronics that can detect any radioactive emissions from a mass of U-235."

"How do they do that?" she asked.

"The vans carried single megacycle detection devices equipped with oscillators that enabled them to pick up, analyze and quantify the smallest measure of radioactive emitted radiation given off by the U-235 inside the recovered

118

nuclear bomb. Hand-held attache cases were also being used by special agents walking through office buildings and business districts to electronically sweep suspected hiding locations without alerting the public. Agent operators were well trained to recognize the U-235 radioactive isotopes from other similar active elements that are used in industrial process manufacturing," said Iron Hand.

As he was outlining the wire tapping operation and its potential to break open more clues, Sara interrupted.

"Hey, boss. We just received some sobering news. The New York City FBI office has received a second express letter from the Islamic Brotherhood in London."

"Go ahead and read it to me, please," said Iron Hand.

"OK. Here's what it says," said Sara.

"The US government is being told to begin wiring the $5 billion in twenty-four hours to their bank in the Netherlands Antilles, Curacao. If they don't receive the funds the Islamic terrorists threaten to detonate their reconfigured atomic bomb within a metropolitan area in the US. Enclosed inside the express mail package was a brass ID plate that contained various military and AEC serial numbers," said Sara.

Sara added, "It is obvious that the brass ID plate strongly suggests the Islamic Brotherhood cell has recovered the lost Air Force bomb and they control the weapons grade U-235. I can pass this along, the ID plate was extremely unsettling to the White House. The assessment here in Langley is that the President is getting big-time pressure from his domestic political advisors to issue an emergency evacuation order for Savannah. The White House is crafting a believable story because they aren't prepared to go public with the news that an Islamic terrorist cell has an atomic

119

bomb ready to explode in downtown Savannah. The cover story will probably be about some large tanker that has been discovered with a highly explosive cargo in its hold. Tighman told me to pass along that there must be some solid progress or news from Operation Blue Shield in twenty-four hours or the cover story and evacuation order will be issued. Once that order is given, this emergency situation will probably spin out of control. The Federal Reserve Bank has said they are ready to begin wiring the blackmail funds at any time."

"OK. I understand," said Iron Hand.

"I'm sorry I have to unload all this on you at the same time." said Sara.

"Don't worry about that. It's important for me to know what Headquarters is thinking. I have to getting going. Talk to you later," said Iron Hand.

Iron Hand put down the phone. The news from Sara was sinking in and he didn't like the feeling he was getting in his gut. He said to himself, "I can't just sit here and wait for the next phone call. I've got to make something happen. Make it happen, Captain."

After telling the FBI agents to get a car ready, Iron Hand dressed in a pair of light weight khaki trousers. He wore an expensive navy blue golf shirt with a polo logo, long billed baseball type cap and expensive brown Armani running shoes. As he walked out of his Command Post it seemed to be full of humidity as sticky perspiration began to form on his body. He decided it was time to pay a visit to the Captain of Miss Thunderbolt.

The government's long-standing resolve of not negotiating with terrorist demands was being given its most solemn test. He knew that he needed to catch a big break somewhere in the investigation- the sooner the better.

As the car left the Hunter, Iron said to his FBI agents, "Head for the shrimp pier on East River Road. We're going to go see the Captain of Miss Thunderbolt. He may know something about Hall's buddies that will help us track down his killer. I'm getting the feeling that Hall's murder and our terrorist's are definitely linked. If we keep pushing maybe we'll catch a break."

Rogers was a laid-back retired Navy chief petty officer. He worried about his shrimp boat and little else. Since being a widowed bachelor, he chose to live on his boat and spent all the waking hours on general repair work and engine overhaul to keep it ready for long days in the waters off Tybee Island.

"Ahoy, Captain. Can we come aboard? We'd like to talk with you about the Hall murder," said Iron Hand.

"Sure, come aboard," as Rogers waved them aboard.

Iron Hand and his ever-present FBI agents climbed aboard Miss Thunderbolt.

The agents flashed their badges in front Rogers. He took Iron Hand's ID and read it carefully. He only glanced at the other two sets of ID, nodding in their direction.

"What's on your mind, gentlemen?" said Rogers.

Iron Hand began, "We're trying to tie-down some facts and see if we can lay them out into some kind of logical scenario. We have to go with what we have – which isn't too much."

Rogers looked pensively at the three men; his face was sort of saying I've seen lots of guys like you before.

"What do you want to know?" said Rogers.

"Have there been any suspicious characters around the shrimp pier or your boat since the Hall murder?" asked Iron Hand.

Rogers looked at Iron Hand, sighed and said, "Inspector, I was a Navy man for 28 years. I'll be happy to help with anything I know about Hall. Just so you know, men are walking along this pier looking for daily or short term work as strikers. I hired two men right after Hall was murdered. I hadn't seen them before they came around asking for work. They said their names were Allan and Oscar. Probably phony, but I didn't press the issue. They did OK work while they lasted. No better, or any worse, than others I've hired. Like I said, they quit after three days. I never saw them again."

"Can you give us a description of the two men you just told us about?" asked Iron Hand.

"Oh sure, dark skinned, black hair and dark eyes. They claimed to be Hispanic but I think they were more like middle eastern guys, maybe Arabs. One was tougher and did most of the talking. Not too tall, either of them, sort of lean and mean, well built and tough looking, if you know what I mean," Rogers said.

Iron Hand listened to Rogers'. "Here's a card and telephone number. If you ever see these men again, call me right away, day or night. If we needed you to identify these guys would you be willing to do it?"

"Sure, I'd be glad to help. Just let me know," said Rogers.

As they walked off the pier Iron Hand said to his FBI agents, "Why did the terrorists give us seven days to meet their demands. Why not three or four days? Maybe because we are dealing with amateurs. Someone or something wasn't in place. They needed time to set-up the bomb perhaps. Get someone here to do the job. This isn't smart. They should have gotten it all ready and set-up before they hit us with the threat letter. Maybe we are dealing with first timers?"

*   *   *   *

Iron Hand and his agents were in their car with the engine running still parked in the lot near the shrimp pier. Iron Hand was figuring his next move when his ringing cell phone snapped Iron Hand back to reality.

"Yes." Iron Hand listened as FBI agents said they had intercepted a call on Abdul's phone. It was traced to a pay telephone in a downtown shopping area. FBI agents were immediately dispatched to the pay telephone location but they arrived too late to grab the caller. To the listening FBI agents, it was obvious that Abdul recognized the caller's voice as he instructed him to go to the Monterey Square for a meeting at 2:00 P.M. Abdul confirmed that he understood the message. After Abdul's confirmation, the line immediately went dead. The FBI reported that no other phone or computer activity was detected from his apartment phone since the wire tap was in place.

*   *   *   *

Iron Hand called Paulson at his marine salvage company.

"Deane-san, have you heard any news through your net work of competitors?"

Paulson replied, "I still have a few messages out and as yet unanswered. I have learned that a middle eastern Arab-looking guy was shopping around for a fifty foot vessel to charter for scuba diving around Tybee Island. The description I have received from my business contacts fits Sherry's boy friend. I can't make a definite connection but I think I'm real close. Wait a minute. Someone handed me a note. This is the news we want. Ten days ago, a forty three-foot Sabreliner was chartered to Abdul Rahman by a marine outfit on the Wellington River. I know this company. They are struggling to remain in business. Apparently, they needed some cash flow and with no other business prospects, Rahman's offer was too good to pass up. The name on the boat is Serious Business. I remember when we were on that shrimp dock last night there was a forty-three footer tied up at the south end but I didn't catch the name. That could be the boat. It certainly fits the description I was given. I suggest you tell the Coast Guard to check out that boat with a search warrant this morning. I can meet you there or stay here and keep digging for more information about Rahman. Your call, Captain."

"Deane-san, your are a jewel among men. Stay where you are and keep up the good work. You have my number. Call me immediately if you get anything more."

In less than five minutes they were standing next to the 43 foot Sabreliner tied to the shrimp pier. The name on the transom read, Serious Business.

Iron Hand used his cell phone, called the local FBI agent in charge to obtain an emergency boarding and search warrant so they could legally check out Serious Business. If the warrant issuance became a problem, the Coast Guard would have to pull an emergency inspection of the vessel on a trumped-up suspected violation.

Anyone found aboard the vessel must be considered to be armed and dangerous. Iron Hand looked at his FBI agents and said,

"Maybe, just maybe, we're starting to get lucky."

Chapter XI

Savannah, Ga.

Iron Hand and two FBI agents stood on the pier next to Serious Business. He decided that he wouldn't wait very long for a court order to authorize a legal boarding of this vessel. If it turned out this was in fact the boat Abdul Rahman had charted for scuba diving it could yield valuable clues for the investigation.

The boat appeared unoccupied but a terrorist might be hiding below deck and the situation had to be considered dangerous. Iron Hand positioned one agent at the head of the pier to watch and stop, if necessary, any civilian who came toward Serious Business while they searched the boat. There was no need to provoke a dispute with anyone who claimed they owned the boat and might question why law enforcement people were onboard.

As Iron Hand stood on Serious Business his mind flashed back to the message about Abdul going to Monterey Square for a meeting with the mysterious caller. He flipped up the cell phone cover and contacted the FBI agents staked out at Abdul's apartment building.

"Listen up, men. Do not, repeat not, make any move against Rahman as he travels to Monterey Square. Do not make any moves against any person that approaches him. I feel this may be a dry run to determine if Abdul's telephone has been bugged. These Islamic terrorists may be smarter than we credit them. Stay well away from Rahman. Our hope is that someone will meet him and lead us to the bomb. Our priority is to find out where the bomb is hidden. Keep me informed if anyone shows up to meet Abdul. Do you copy?"

"Roger, Iron Hand."

*   *   *   *

Ahmad gritted his jaw as he cut off the cell phone circuit. He thought that the telephone sounded hollow and different. This feeling was unsettling. Ahmad sensed that the American security may have identified Abdul and zeroed in on his phone line. There could be other investigations being conducted behind the scene that Abdul wouldn't know about. Ahmad decided his safest move would be to observe Abdul in Monterey square from a safe distance and then follow him after he left. Ahmad wouldn't take any unnecessary risks at this crucial point of the mission. Ahmad felt good that his sensory defenses had kicked-in to ward off any chance encounter with the police or the FBI.

Ahmad turned his attention to Bruslov. "Sergei, you remain confident the bomb will function properly in twenty-four hours?"

"Yes, I have rechecked my calculations and all is in order. I estimate a blast effect of seven kilo-tons of TNT, more than enough to completely destroy the entire waterfront and three miles around ground zero."

Ahmad displayed a small smile as he digested this final assessment from his nuclear technician. Bruslov was attempting to reassure Ahmad that he was totally dedicated to accomplishing the mission. Bruslov guessed that Ahmad and Omar probably planned to draw the American security forces away from the warehouse in a diversionary confrontation. Some last noble shoot-out or stand off would

126

guarantee them martyr's glory within the Islamic Brotherhood.

As a way of testing his theory Bruslov asked Ahmad,

"What are your plans for evacuating the blast area?" Bruslov watched Ahmad's reaction to his question. He wanted to gauge the response because it would pertain to his own survival chances after the bomb was operational and the timing device was set to count-down.

Ahmad wasted no time with pleasantries, "We will take our boat down the Florida Inter-Coastal waterway and, if Allah is willing, make our way to the Grand Bahama Islands." Bruslov nodded his approval playing the role of a loyal team member, willingly accepting Ahmad's plan for their escape from ground zero. Bruslov had been in the warehouse so long his clothes, body and hair were reeking of smelly machine oil, and all the musty odors of an old dirty shop. He longed for a clean hotel room, a hot bath and a decent meal. Actually, the last thing that Bruslov planned was to go aboard the boat used to recover the bomb. In Bruslov's mind, there was no way the boat would be capable of out-running the Coast Guard and certainly it was too big to blend into a harbor without being noticed by suspicious American security forces.

Bruslov walked up to Ahmad and said, "I am now ready to start the count-down on the timing device. I need to know when you want the bomb to detonate?"

"Set the bomb to explode at 12:00 midnight. If you start the count-down now we will have eleven hours and thirty minutes to clear the blast area. I want the bomb to explode at night because I believe that will cause even more panic."

Ahmad stepped away and conferred with Omar and Majed. He then announced,

"I must leave to meet my brother. I'll return in forty-five minutes."

Bruslov continued to hover around the bomb, stalling and pretending to be making last minute adjustments to the timing device. Majed seemed interested in this process and closely watched what Bruslov was doing to the bomb. Bruslov had long since stopped worrying about Majed's nosey intrusions.

Food was ordered from a local fast food restaurant as had been their practice since occupying the warehouse. Always the same dreadful meals: Mexican tamales and fried beans with spiced rice, served with soft drinks or tea. After the meal arrived, it was quickly consumed.

Ahmad had been gone for about ten minutes driving alone to Monterey Square for his two o'clock meeting with his brother. With the timing device now set and counting down the twelve hours until the detonation, Bruslov felt this was probably his last opportunity to escape. With Ahmad not present to complicate his departure, his chances of success were much higher. Bruslov said to Omar,

"I need to use the toilet. This lunch isn't settling well with me." Bruslov headed for the toilet. Bruslov had barely touched his Mexican food but made a show of tasting everything.

Bruslov closed the bathroom door. He immediately opened the black-painted window, climbed out feet first, and eased himself quietly to the ground. He was confident no one could see him making his escape. Bruslov estimated he had five or six minutes head start before Omar would come looking in the toilet. Then another two minutes while he searched the warehouse and outside the grounds to find him. Bruslov figured he had eight minutes max before the entire terrorist team could begin searching for him. Bruslov guessed Omar would immediately contact Ahmad and alert him to his disappearance. Ahmad and his brother could then choose: search the streets or head to the boat for their exit from ground zero.

As Bruslov jogged at a slow pace down the road, he knew that he could not run all the way into town. His mind was searching for a sensible way to escape from the neighborhood. He had to keep moving at all costs. He pictured Omar and the others racing down the road behind with guns under their shirts ready to kill him on sight for leaving the warehouse without permission.

Bruslov got lucky. A city bus came along its route to pick up waiting passengers at the next corner; Bruslov boarded the bus, not caring where it was headed. As long as the bus could take him out of the area, anywhere was acceptable. As the bus started to make turns toward downtown Bruslov relaxed for the first time in three days. Perhaps, if his luck continued, he could get off the bus in the downtown area, duck into a restaurant for some decent food, call his taxi-driver friend whose telephone number he had memorized, and go to the airport terminal. As the bus traveled through the Savannah streets, Bruslov checked his pocket to be sure he hadn't lost his airport locker key in all the excitement.

*   *   *   *

Abdul sat on a park bench in the Monterey Square underneath the beautiful live oak trees. The weather was warm and humid but this heat was nothing compared to what he had known in Cairo and grown used to as a young man.

Abdul had his hand on his cell phone. He battled within himself over the risk of compromising the mission by calling Sherry. He desperately wanted to tell her to leave Savannah with her child and travel to Orlando and visit the Disney park for several days. As his mind continued to focus, he realized that Ahmad would be arriving shortly and he didn't want to be forced to explain why he was talking on his cell phone. He decided he could say he was checking if his home phone was working. Abdul dialed Sherry's number.

Sherry was home and preparing to go to work. She was surprised to hear from Abdul as he had been distant with her for almost a week. She had not seen him for almost five days after their last session of making love at his apartment. Sherry listened to Abdul making his points with his voice in a highly agitated state.

"Abdul, what are you talking about? Why is it so important that I travel to Florida today? I think it's wonderful that you are offering to do this but, what is going on?"

Abdul became frustrated and said abruptly, "Please don't argue. Just do this one thing for me. I can't talk much longer. We may not see each other again. If it is possible, I will explain everything later." Abdul cut off the connection and jammed the cell phone deep into his pocket.

*   *   *   *

Suddenly Bruslov was shocked to see Abdul sitting on a park bench as the CAT bus made its way around the streets lining Monterey Square. For a moment Bruslov was frozen in fear that Ahmad would be close by and see him riding alone on the bus. By this time Omar had surely alerted Ahmad that he had escaped. If they could find him, they would kill him without hesitation. Bruslov slouched down in his seat and peered out the bus windows to see if he could locate Ahmad's car parked near Monterey Square. Abdul remained seated on the park bench and looked apprehensive

130

as if something was wrong. Bruslov slouched down further in his seat; picked up a discarded newspaper, and pretended to be reading as he hid himself from the bus window. Bruslov thought for a split second that his luck had run out. Now all he thought of was getting off the bus in the crowded streets and disappearing into a restaurant. His stomach was turning into knots with fear.

Something had obviously happened with the meeting between Ahmad and Abdul. Had his escape from the warehouse triggered a major problem? Why was Abdul sitting in the park alone? The CAT shuttle bus moved along East Gaston past several other squares and turned south on Habersham street. Bruslov got off the bus on East Hall street and looked for a restaurant. Anything would be fine. He had to get off the streets. People seemed to be milling around but no one paid any attention to his movements, for which he was happy. He could feel the sweat begin to run down his back. He tried to stay on the shady side of the street and watched for door ways to duck into if it became necessary. All his survival senses were working but he was anxious to get into some cover and regroup his mind. He was glad that he had spent some time walking through the City the first day he arrived in Savannah. He did not feel completely lost now because of that well spent time.

As Sergei walked down the shady sidewalk he spotted a seafood restaurant that seemed quiet. Sergei walked in the restaurant and headed directly to a back booth. Two men in the next booth were loudly discussing the loss of waiters who had quit their jobs on their cruise ship. Bruslov overhead them saying good waiters were hard to replace in ports of call. Bruslov listened carefully as he waited for a waiter to take his food order of fried shrimp and hushpuppies. Ice tea was served with lots of sweetener. Bruslov gulped downed the first glass of ice tea and signaled he wanted more. He noticed his body was beginning to cool down and his mind began to relax from his escapade. Sergei thought for a moment, perhaps he could take a job as a cruise ship waiter and leave it when the ship was in New York City, or some foreign port. There would be no problem using his fake ID and passport. Suddenly his mind snapped. What was he thinking? His nuclear bomb was due to destroy the harbor in less than eleven hours. Sergei dismissed this idea and realized he was not thinking clearly.

Sergei finished his shrimp dinner and paid the bill. He telephone his taxi driver and waited just inside the door. When the cab pulled up in front of the restaurant Sergei jumped in the back door and slouched down. He said, "Airport terminal, please," trying not to appear that he was near panic. The taxi driver tried to be friendly but Bruslov did not feel like getting into a spirited conversation. Actually, Bruslov was not sure the driver remembered him from his earlier cab ride. That would be fine. When you are on the run, the fewer people who remember you, the better. Bruslov slouched into the back seat and pretended to be napping.

The taxi ride to the airport terminal seemed to take an eternity but the trip was accomplished in twenty minutes with a several stops at traffic lights. Sergei entered the terminal and sat down on the first row of seats to get his bearings. He observed that there no security men watching for anyone or hanging around the rental lockers. A cleaning person was sweeping up dirt in the far end of the area. After five minutes of watching the terminal activity, he approached his rented locker and retrieved his disguise and extra clothes. He retreated to the men's room and found the disabled toilet stall available. Bruslov entered it and changed his clothes and entire appearance; hair piece, different shoes, pants, baseball cap and light weight jacket.

During the taxi ride Bruslov had been rolling over his escape options in his mind. He needed to plan his next moves very carefully. He asked himself, "Should I take a plane from Savannah since I'm already in the airport." He checked the departure board. The next plane going north wouldn't leave for three hours. This would be too big of a gamble to stay around the airport that long. Security forces could be alerted if something went wrong back at the warehouse and he would be stuck in a waiting room. The airport would be the first place security forces would check out for suspicious people. He kept saying to himself, "I have to keep moving."

His second option was bus transportation out of Savannah to Charlotte, North Carolina and then a plane up to New York City. He picked up a public telephone and called the bus terminal. "What is the next bus departure to Columbia or any city up north?" asked Bruslov.

"The next bus leaves for Charlotte, North Carolina in thirty five minutes. There are plenty of seats available," said the ticket clerk.

"Thank you. I will want a one-way ticket to Charlotte. I am leaving right now to catch that bus."

Bruslov now needed transportation back downtown to the bus terminal. This was not a problem as there were many taxis waiting for fares just outside the airport building. Although this trip to the airport was bothersome it served the purpose of getting him away from Ahmad and the other terrorist team members who were certainly searching for him and anxious to kill him. Bruslov walked to the taxi stand area and signaled he wanted a taxi.

"Please take me to the bus station in Savannah. How much will it cost and how long will it take?" said Bruslov as he climbed into the taxi. He already knew the answers but he wanted to appear normal to the driver and mask his anxiety.

The Savannah bus terminal was a mixed crowd of people sleeping in waiting seats, young people with children huddled in travel seats, and old persons heading back to their homes looking for the cheapest transportation available. Fast food was served in the back rooms to those who wanted some hamburgers and fries before boarding a bus for their destinations.

Upon his arrival, Sergei went to the men's room and neatly re-folded his clothes into his small carry-on soft luggage bag. He doubled checked his appearance in the mirror, left the men's room and approached the ticket windows.

"One way ticket to Charlotte, North Carolina, please," Bruslov said in his best English.

"OK. That will be $35. The bus leaves in ten minutes from gate six."

"Fine. Thank you."

Bruslov went to the waiting benches and sat in the last seat of a vacant row. He kept a sharp eye on the front door for police or security forces and one eye on the large wall clock. Sergei was thankful he had eaten in a decent restaurant before coming to the bus terminal. The announcement soon came.

"All aboard for Charlotte, North Carolina, and points North."

Sergei boarded the bus slowly, selected a seat in the back row and buried his face in a newspaper.

*   *   *   *

Iron Hand and one FBI agent approached the forty-three foot boat with caution, but determined easily that there was no one on board. They boarded Serious Business and began a careful search of the spaces and cabin areas. The boat interior was clean, everything seem ship shape. Iron Hand noted the fuel gauges were registering almost full.

"Check every trash receptacle and drawer. Something left behind might lead us to them," Iron Hand said in his best command voice.

"I want to install several tracking bugs in case they take her out and we miss that move," said Iron Hand.

"That will be no problem. We have two electronic bugs in our car trunk. We can have them installed in ten minutes," said the agent.

"Get on it right away. We don't want to be here too long."

Time was getting tight. Iron Hand knew he needed a break but didn't know where it was going to come from.

"Call being patched in from the base for you, Iron Hand. Caller says she is Sherry Norwood. She says it's important."

Iron Hand picked up the cell phone and said, "Hello, Sherry. I hope you have something for me. We're running out of time and good leads."

"Abdul just called and told me to leave town immediately. He said he may never see me again. He sounded very nervous and confused. He would not discuss anything in detail. Just get out of town as soon as possible. What does all this mean? What do you think I should do?"

Iron Hand thought quickly. If he told her the truth and she repeated the story to others the entire community of

Savannah would panic. Iron Hand answered her in his most reassuring voice,

"Don't panic. I believe that Abdul is deeply involved in this murder of the shrimp boat crewman and he is feeling guilty. If you know anything more, now is the time to tell me."

"I told you everything I know. There is no sense in me attempting to make up stories about Abdul," said Sherry with a little bark in her voice.

"I will call you if I hear anything new about this situation." said Iron Hand. He put the phone down and thought that the situation is getting critical and about to spin out of control.

*   *   *   *

Ahmad was sitting in his car when the call came through on his cell phone. He immediately sensed something had gone wrong when the phone started ringing. Omar explained that Bruslov had disappeared and was nowhere to be found.

"Omar, how did Sergei get away from you and Majed?" Omar knew he had failed Ahmad but he did not feel guilty. "Sergei excused himself to visit the toilet and never returned." This was the simple truth. What else could he say?

"The bomb remains armed, in good shape, and the timing device is running perfectly. The time left until the detonation was approximately ten hours and twenty minutes," said Omar as he scrambled to reassure Ahmad that everything else was satisfactory.

"Omar, prepare everything for a speedy departure as soon as I return. I must get Abdul and bring him along.

136

Recheck the timing device and leave everything else alone. When the detonation occurs there will be nothing left."

"Everything will be done as you have ordered."

Ahmad listened and cut off the connection. He turned his attention to Abdul who was getting up from his park bench and walking toward his car. Ahmad drove around the square and went into an alley that Abdul had to pass on his way to his car. Ahmad got out of his car and ran back fifty feet to the sidewalk and motioned to Abdul to follow him.

"There are problems. The Russian traitor Bruslov has deserted us and we cannot find him. Omar tells me the bomb is safe and the timer is functioning. In less than ten hours the Americans will learn about what it is like to be bombed in their own country." Ahmad looked at his brother Abdul and did not like the expression he saw on his face. "What's the matter? Are you getting too soft in your old age?" Abdul turned and said to Ahmad, "Yes, I am soft. I do not like all this killing. I wanted to help you with the mission, but now I'm scared that the authorities are going to close in and we will be captured and spend our remaining lives rotting in some American jail." Adbul was starting to come unraveled. Ahmad could feel the sense of hopelessness in his brother's voice.

Ahmad drove as fast as he could back to the warehouse without bringing attention to his driving. Ahmad picked up his cell phone and called Omar.

"Prepare everything for an immediate departure. I am about five minutes from you. Double-check the apparatus and timing device. I will make one final inspection of the warehouse," said Ahmad.

Omar again said, "Everything is in order. We await your arrival."

*   *   *   *

Bruslov began to review his plan to elude the American security forces, whom by now, were certainly searching for him. He retraced his action after escaping from the warehouse; he had left behind his tool case and instruments used to work on the bomb. Did he leave any obvious clues inside the tool case that compromised his identity? Not that he remembered. Were his fingerprints going to be found on the tools and instruments? Yes, but would the Americans think the tools belonged to Ahmad and Omar? What about his clothing and personal items left in the machine shop? He had cut out the clothing labels so as not to leave a trail back to London.

If the Americans captured any of the terrorists alive, could they piece together his identity through them? Maybe, if a solid offer of clemency was presented so they could avoid long jail terms. Bruslov forced himself to stop thinking about what might happen. There were too many possibilities.

As the bus rolled along, Bruslov calculated there were less than nine hours remaining before the bomb detonated. Of course, this assumed that the security forces had not discovered the building and the bomb. In two more hours he should be well past Columbia and on to his next destination, Charlotte. Bruslov told himself it was smart he had purchased a one-way ticket. He could change his appearance again in the Columbia bus terminal if there was some lay-over time.

The faster he put distance between himself and Savannah the better. Suddenly, fatigue overcame him and he had the sinking feeling that the whole mission was probably compromised. His mind was exhausted and the droning bus engine made him sleepy. As he nodded off, his hand checked his pocket for his fake passport and wallet. He reminded himself, "My name is David Dickinson."

"Hey, buddy. You'al gettin' off at Columbia?" was all that Bruslov heard as the man in the next seat shook his shoulder. "We got five more minutes before we arrive at the bus terminal." Bruslov smiled, and said, "Yes, thanks for waking me."

Bruslov got off the bus and looked around for a convenient restroom to change his appearance and clean up. He was sick of smelly buses and greasy fried food.

A good meal at a restaurant was also something that would make him feel better. He stood in front of a newsstand and read the newspaper headlines.

"What are you looking for pal?" asked the attendant.

"I want the latest newspapers. Which of these are the most recent?"

Bruslov paid for two papers and tucked them under his arm. The headlines told nothing about a terrorist plot or bomb threat. For this, he was thankful. Perhaps there would be more time before his description was posted in the papers. Bruslov figured he was 100 miles from Savannah – not far enough. He wanted to get moving. He worked his way over to the ticket window and rechecked the schedule for the departure to Charlotte. He tried to act calm and normal.

"The bus leaves in fifteen minutes from dock number seven," an attendant said to Bruslov. He then retreated to a row of seats for waiting passengers. With the stopping, starting and traffic jams he had been on the run for about four hours. He did not want to be trapped on the parked bus in case some law enforcement people started moving through the bus terminal. He scanned the papers further and found nothing about a bomb threat or any news about Savannah.

Satisfied that he was safe, Bruslov headed for the men's room to freshen up and wash the grime off his hands and face. He sat in a toilet stall for five minutes to give himself some privacy. Mentally he said, "It's time to refocus and remember what he was up against." He got up, left the restroom and headed to the food counter.

"Give me a burger, fries and Coca Cola," said Bruslov. Bruslov sat at a dirty table and his thoughts drifted back to the warehouse. He tried to imagine what had happened. Had the terrorist escaped in the boat as Ahmad had planned? Would Ahmad lead the terrorist team into a fight with the police to draw them away from the bomb? Were they all dead? That would be the best scenario if he were to elude the police. It was impossible to speculate further. The most important thing for him was to keep traveling and blend into the American society as he headed north. If he could reach a Russian community within a large metropolitan area, he might get some peace and find time to organize a trip back to London. He had often heard, "Brighton Beach in New York City was the home to many Russian immigrates. Toronto was another city that had plenty of Russians."

*   *   *   *

When Ahmad arrived in the cinder covered parking lot of the warehouse the building looked deserted. He said to Abdul, "Stay in the car and I will come back in a few minutes." Ahmad was furious that Bruslov had escaped from the team and was now loose and out of his control. One wrong move by Bruslov and the entire mission would certainly be compromised. Ahmad had thought of nothing since hearing that Bruslov had left the building, except getting even with the Russian. He decided he would plant incriminating information next to the bomb which would implicate Bruslov to the FBI if the bomb failed to detonate. If the bomb exploded, the information about Bruslov would be lost in the blast. As Ahmad opened the door to the building Omar and Majed were ready to leave. "Everything is in good order," said Omar. Ahmad nodded and said, "Go to the truck and get ready to drive to our boat." As they left the building, Ahmad opened a small brief case he had hidden in the building. It contained a complete dossier of Bruslov provided to him by the London al-Qaeda headquarters.

Ahmad walked toward the bomb and checked the ticking timing device. He could plainly see there was less than ten hours remaining on the clock. Everything seemed to be working perfectly, just as Omar had said. Ahmad placed the picture of Bruslov and his file that the London al-Qaeda organization had given him. If the bomb somehow failed to explode, it would be impossible not to find the dossier of Bruslov. He would be blamed for the work restoring the bomb. He would be tracked down by the US government law enforcement agencies. Assuming that Ahmad and the remaining team escaped the law authorities, Ahmad would communicate to London that Bruslov had disobeyed orders and deserved to be eliminated. Certainly no more payments should be paid to Bruslov. Ahmad promised to himself, he would kill Bruslov on the spot if he ever found him.

Ahmad looked once more at the bomb and the countdown device. He was satisfied. He turned, left the building, locked the doors from the outside and climbed into the truck. Ahmad looked at the men and said,

"Drive to our boat. We are done with this phase of our mission."

The other Muslims said, "Praise Allah."

Chapter XII

Don Kramer had been a FBI agent for five years. Counter terrorist duty was his most exciting work assignment. In Operation Blue Shield, Kramer led a four man team of agents assigned to drive unmarked vans equipped with ultra sensitive CRT scopes designed to track down electron emissions from radioactive U-235.

During the first two days of patrolling Savannah, no emission readings were detected. On their third day of the operation, Kramer's team was going to check out the waterfront district and three miles south of the port.

Kramer graduated from Michigan State University with an accounting degree. Next he earned a law degree at the University of Detroit and interviewed with FBI recruiters in the old Detroit Federal Building on West Lafayette. He liked the sense of order, purpose and discipline the FBI represented. For Kramer, tracking down the criminals and other bad guys for the FBI would never be a problem.

"Go back down this street again before we head over to the waterfront. Another team has already been here, but let's check it out again," said Kramer.

After ten minutes of normal readings, an agent operator received one long loud ping reading on his scope. "Got a solid reading coming in at nine o'clock. Definitely not industrial ground clutter"

"Mark that bearing. Let's go around again for another reading to confirm it," said Kramer. He thought, just maybe, we're going to hit the jackpot. "Coming around now, we should be getting solid readings right about now if the first one was the real."

"Bingo."

"We have a second confirmation reading loud and clear. Must be coming from that old brick warehouse building off to the left. Looks like an old garage or machine shop; No visible signs of any inside activity. The parking lot is empty."

Kramer's pulse rate jumped; his usual calmness gave way to real excitement, as he sensed that perhaps some action was coming up.

"Pull into the parking lot and lock on that bearing. Tell me again what you are getting," said Kramer.

"If this isn't U-235 or U-238 I'd like to know what it is?" stated the agent.

"I'm reporting to the Command Post with our exact location and time of the discovery. We will have to wait until we get back-up units before entering the building," said Kramer. Kramer could feel the excitement in his voice as he read their position to the Command Post operator at Hunter army airfield: 101 West Victory Drive; just east of the intersection with Banard Street. The parking lot was full of rubble and cinders, barely functional but still usable. The building was in need of paint and general repair; all the windows had been painted black with cheap spray-can paint. A painted sign was hanging crookedly and gave the name of the business operating inside: Ajax Waste & Recycling, Inc. A small sign tacked below said: No Hiring Today.

"Captain. This is Hunter Command Post. We have a positive reading of U-235 coming from inside a building at 101 West Victory Drive. Back-up units are on the way to assist agent Kramer's team. They are waiting in the driveway until the back-up units arrive. The building appears to be deserted. Can I pass along any orders?"

"Command Post. This is McQuesten. I copy your last. We are heading over to the Victory Drive location. Issue orders for all units to proceed to the Victory Drive address. If this is the bomb, and it would seem so, order our disposal teams to this location. Also, contact the local police; get a Swat Team into the area to stand by for my orders. Patch me through to flight operations control at Marine Air Station, Beaufort."

"Roger, Captain. Please stand by."

Moments later a cool voice of an experienced flight operation controller came on to Iron Hand's cell phone line.

"Flight operations control, Beaufort."

"Flight operations control, this is Captain McQuesten, Commander of Operation Blue Shield. Please advise your readiness status."

"Roger, Captain. We have three F-18's on runway alert status. Three pilots are in the ready room, briefed and standing by. Also, two helicopters with fifty marines are standing by for lift-off instructions. They could be airborne in twenty minutes, or less. Once airborne, the ETA of the marines in Savannah is twenty minutes.

The F-18's can be overhead in six minutes."

"Roger, your last Flight Ops. Launch three F-18's immediately for a low-level fly-by. Bump up the next three to Runway Alert. Give me a fly-by over Tybee Island and down over Wassaw Sound. Have this repeated twice and then climb to 5,000 feet and orbit three miles out to sea," ordered Iron Hand.

"Roger, Captain. Do you anticipate a weapons release? If so, we require a code from you authorizing weapons release once airborne over Tybee Island."

"Roger, Flight Ops. Code for weapons release by F-18's is as follows: Bravo Lima or, Blue Light. Repeat: Blue Light."

"Roger, Captain. Those code words check out with our instructions. Three F-18's now in roll out and airborne in one minute. Roger Out."

Iron Hand clicked off his cell phone. He thought to himself, if those terrorist bastards are out there maybe our show of military muscle will shake them up and they'll do something stupid.

*   *   *   *

Ahmad and Omar drove toward River Road to get aboard their boat, Serious Business. Abdul sat low in the back seat hoping that no one by chance would see him and wonder what he was doing. As their car approached the parking area off River Road, everything seemed normal. Ahmad turned from the front seat, looked at Abdul, and said,

"Go down to the boat alone, and open it up. Signal back an all-clear sign if it is safe for us to come aboard."

As Abdul approached Serious Business, he glanced toward Tubby's. He wondered if Sherry had failed to understand his pleading and was in Savannah. Women can be so hard to deal with sometimes, thought Abdul. He climbed aboard Serious Business and found the boat free of any law enforcement agents. He raised his hands and signaled to the others to join him.

Once aboard Serious Business, Ahmad took command. "Omar, start up the engines and cast off immediately," said Ahmad. Abdul sensed this was probably his last time to see Savannah. Again, he looked toward Tubby's to see if Sherry was visible. He snapped back to reality and began to dutifully carryout Ahmad's orders. He resigned himself that he probably would not survive this trip and stopped worrying about his possessions in his apartment. His life in Savannah and this world was finished.

The twin engines rumbled up, coughed several times and began to turn-over in perfect harmony. Ahmad ordered Majed to cast off all lines and go below and breakout all the charts for a southerly passage on the Inter-Coastal waterway. Omar maneuvered the boat into the Wilmington River and started a smooth run out to Wassaw Sound. Omar was being careful not to make any heavy wake in the narrow channel. Making their get-away in an unobtrusive manner was critical.

Serious Business responded smartly to his movements of the controls. Ahmad and Omar looked up at the three American jets as they flew low over Tybee Island off to their portside. Omar mentally estimated the jets were at a range of four miles. Ahmad grumbled to Omar, "The dirty infidel Americans are looking for trouble; they will get it when our bomb detonates."

*   *   *   *

Paulson steered his thirty-eight foot Sea Ray cruiser into the waters south of Tybee Island. He planned to come up the Wilmington River and dock where Serious Business was moored. Paulson had been in Wassaw Sound for two hours. His yacht, Game Bird, came to life nicely as he pushed up the rpm's for a short speed run. Seated in the flying bridge he felt an adrenaline rush as the wind ran through his thinning hair. Paulson felt he could do more from his yacht to assist McQuesten than sitting behind a desk at his salvage company. He brought along his old .45 Colt automatic from his flying days. He couldn't remember the last time he had fired it. As he entered the mouth of the Wilmington River, Paulson figured there was about thirty feet of water under the keel as long as he stayed in the center of the channel. Turner Creek lay to starboard with Dutch Island coming up on the port side. He reduced the engine rpm's to cut back the wake he was churning up.

Paulson didn't see the jets, but he heard the thunder of the F-18's as they did a low-level pass over the outer edges of Tybee Island. Paulson sensed they were too low for practice. He also wondered if McQuesten was behind this display of Marine aviation muscle. The F-18 jets flew straight out, well past Wassaw Island, then snap-rolled perfectly to port and did a slow turning maneuver that brought them back around to their original heading; then they came back up north toward the Savannah River. Paulson estimated their altitude at eight hundred feet max, a little too low for practice, maybe this was the real deal Iron Hand had hinted about over dinner.

All this Blue Angels action caused Paulson to drift off his course heading. His real job was not to ram Game Bird into another boat or run aground. He forced himself not to look at the jets. As he settled back into the business of piloting his yacht up the Wilmington River, he noticed a forty three foot yacht coming down the channel. As the oncoming boat got closer, Paulson raised his glasses and checked out the bridge area. He saw two dark skinned Arab type men that were nervously jumping around the pilot house and bridge. My God, is that boat Serious Business? Paulson asked himself. If it is, then these could be the bad guys that McQuesten wants to apprehend.

As the two vessels passed port side to port, Paulson did his best to appear nonchalant about what was happening aboard the Sabreliner. As they headed out the channel, Paulson swung around his glasses to look at the transom of the passing boat; he focused the lens on the boat's name: Serious Business.

The next instant Paulson picked up his cell phone to call the number McQuesten had given him for an emergency. Paulson had written the number on a piece of paper and taped it to his cell phone. The Command Post operator answered his call after one ring. "This is Paulson. I'm a navy shipmate of Captain McQuesten's.

He gave me this to call in an emergency. I'm on the Wassaw Sound in my boat Game Bird. Get word to McQuesten that Serious Business just passed me heading out to sea on a southerly course doing about eighteen knots. Two dark skinned Arab types are piloting her. Get this information to McQuesten. Put me on hold and tell me what he says."

Paulson was on hold for what seemed like ten minutes but actually only two. The operator came back on the line; "Captain McQuesten says to tail Serious Business from a safe distance. The men aboard are armed and dangerous. Do not make any effort to engage them. He will call you back. Please advise us your cell phone number and keep the line open." Paulson thought this was just like being in a war movie.

"OK. I'll stick to them from about one and a half miles." Paulson told himself this was not the time to get cute and become a dead hero. Paulson maintained his present course until there was a two mile gap between his yacht and Serious Business; then he rolled over the helm to port and Game Bird smartly answered his command.

In approximately two minutes he was trailing in the wake of Serious Business. Paulson was able to sneak several looks into the pilot house of Serious Business and it appeared that the men were not aware of his maneuver to slip in behind them. As long as Paulson was able to keep Serious Business in his line of sight he made no attempt to close in on the boat. A distance of 1-1/2 miles or a little less was just fine. Paulson kept wondering if he was going to get some help from the Coast Guard or Marine helicopters.

Unconsciously his right hand kept going to his Colt .45. His conscious thought was: When will McQuesten get here?

Chapter XIII

Standing in the cinder laden warehouse parking lot with several FBI agents, Iron Hand began to piece together his new information and intelligence. Inside the warehouse, seven bomb squad technicians huddled over the reconfigured bomb. They stared in curiosity at what the terrorists were able to accomplish with the recovered nuclear bomb and its plutonium core. A photographer busily took pictures for their records.

"Who ever jury-rigged this bomb to detonate knew what he was doing," said a technician. "Yeah, the guy is a nuclear bomb artist," said another bomb squad member. "I wonder where he learned how to do this?" said another.

Iron Hand entered the warehouse and walked up to the bomb squad leader. His impatience was starting to bubble over.

"What's taking so long to disarm this thing? I need an all-clear signal so we can air-lift this contraption out of here."

"We're checking carefully how much time remains on the timing device. The clock may be wrong. Also, it's possible there might be a booby trap wire hidden somewhere," said a technician. "The immediate concern is checking the bomb timing device for a booby trap." Iron Hand said, "Yeah. OK," and shook his head up and down in agreement. "Here's some more input that you can pass along," said another technician.

"We've found a suitcase next to the bomb full of instruments that were probably used by the guy who reworked the bomb. At this point, our best guess is that the bomb trigger device would have exploded but it probably wouldn't have been powerful enough to cause fission of the U-235 plutonium core to go nuclear. That's just a guess though. If the bomb had detonated there would have been a dirty bomb explosion, powerful enough to spread U-235 contamination in the immediate area. The tools, instruments and suitcase don't appear to be US manufactured goods, probably European. We're checking everything in the tool case for fingerprints,"

In frustration Iron Hand shouted an order to a FBI agent. "Contact the Command Post and order another chopper from the Marine base to come here so we can lift this bomb to a Coast Guard cutter ten miles out to sea." Iron Hand figured that if there was a foul-up and the bomb detonated at least it wouldn't destroy Savannah.

A technician approached Iron Hand and handed him an envelope full of papers and a photograph. "You'll find this interesting reading. We think this might be information about the guy who reworked the bomb. Looks like we're dealing with a Russian."

Iron Hand read the file hastily and commented, "If this is about the guy who reworked the bomb, there must have been a serious falling-out between the terrorists. Something caused them to leave his dossier where we'd be sure to find it. If the bomb didn't detonate no one could miss finding these papers. My guess is this Bruslov guy has bolted from the group and they are trying to even-up the score. Obviously, these Arab guys don't know the first thing about nuclear weapons or how to rig up the bomb to explode. They had to bring in someone who knew what to do." Iron Hand mused to himself, All our work back at Langley points to Russian KGB and army officers who have defected or left Russia because they are tired low pay and living like peasants. Selling their nuclear know-how for big bucks to some terrorist group fits the scenario we've got on our hands.

Iron Hand let his mind digest this new development and then settled on what action to take. He ordered an East Coast manhunt for a Russian spy. The word 'bomber' must not be used to explain why the Russian was wanted. If the general public thought a Russian was trying to blow up Savannah there could be wide spread panic. He went to his FBI agent and said,

"Listen up. This is critical. Place this man's picture, name and description on the wires immediately. Send an APB to all local and state police plus every FBI field office on the eastern seaboard. This also has to be released to every newspaper, TV and radio station, airports, Greyhound bus terminals and Amtrak stations. We have to grab this Russian guy, Sergei Bruslov. Report back when this is done!"

Iron Hand said to himself, "There's a story about this Russian and I'm going to figure it out."

Bruslov had ridden Greyhound buses five hours dressed in disguise. He went through Columbia without a hitch and the bus was now approaching Charlotte. After arriving in Charlotte, he tentatively planned to go directly to the airport and purchase a ticket on the first available flight to Boston or New York City. He realized this move would be risky, but he was convinced it would be easier to hide in a larger city. So far he hadn't had problems blending into the general public. Mentally, he patted himself on the back over his success at eluding the police. He was growing more confident about his chances of not getting caught. Unfortunately, though, he couldn't shake a nagging feeling that the FBI was alerted to the bomb plot and probably following his trail.

Bruslov reminded himself, he had to get out of his disguise because the fake photo ID cards he had to use when he purchased his airline ticket were of himself and not some disguise. The big question was: "When and where would he discard his disguise?" He rolled this question over in his mind. He needed time to think things through. When was the next flight leaving Charlotte for Boston or New York City? How much time did he have before he needed to change his appearance? Should he arrive at the airport in disguise or should he get out of his disguise now? This could be critical to his chances of survival.

As he left the Charlotte bus terminal he walked the streets until he spotted a Starbucks coffee shop. He entered the coffee shop, bought a large serving of regular blend black plus a bagel and sat down in a quiet corner table. Bruslov thought to himself, thank goodness the counter girl didn't say anything other than thank-you. He was sick of hearing, "Have a Nice Day."

Bruslov picked up a discarded newspaper and scanned it for news about a bomb scare in Savannah. Nothing was reported. "Are these the latest papers?" he asked himself. Bruslov finished his coffee and bagel. He made his decision. He would go to the airport wearing his disguise, check the flight departure boards, and then change back to his real identity in the men's restroom. He had carefully calculated the time to be required waiting near the departure gate before the flight. As he was about to leave for the men's room he scanned the coffee shop for anyone who might have an eye on him. Nothing set-off his internal defense alarm. Even the smallest slip-up at this point could spell disaster. Bruslov left the coffee shop, walked slowly to blend in with the people on the sidewalk and began looking for a taxi.

A taxi stand had a single cab waiting for a fare. Bruslov knocked on the window to wake up the driver. "I want to go to the Charlotte airport. Can you take me?" asked Bruslov. "No problem. Get in," said the driver. "How much will it cost?" asked Bruslov. "About $15 bucks, depending on which terminal," said the cabby. "Fine. Take me to the USAir terminal," said Bruslov.

FBI agent Paul Holder was the senior field agent in the Charlotte office. He wasn't burdened with any office management responsibilities for which he was thankful. There was enough regular paperwork, meetings and general administration with his fieldwork. He didn't relish the thought of some day being told he would have to begin managing other agents and listening to their complaints. "Who needs that routine?" Holder asked himself.

The Office Manager had called an emergency meeting at 5:00 P.M. to review an APB from the Savannah, Georgia office concerning a Russian male fugitive who was wanted and allegedly linked to a bomb threat on the Savannah waterfront. Each agent was given a complete description and photo of the suspect along with orders to approach him carefully. Holder and his partner were assigned to cover the Charlotte airport for the next six hours.

"How do you want to handle the surveillance for this Russian dude?" asked Holder's partner. This job could mean lots of leg-work and the chances of finding this guy is less than 50-50. The key to catching this suspect was to guess where he would first arrive and then guess where his next move would take him. Holder had done this kind of surveillance many times before so it wasn't like he had to reinvent the wheel.

"Let's head over to the taxi stand at the USAirways terminal. We'll speak to every cabby starting from the end of the line and work to the front. Maybe we'll get lucky. If not, we can check out the bus terminal drop off points. Take it slow. Don't get excited," said Holder.

"I like your leadership style," said Holder's partner.

As they walked along the line of cabs, Holder said to his partner, "This Russian dude must be pretty smart if he can work on bombs and then disappear into our society. My

154

guess is we're looking for someone that doesn't look foreign but is more "American" if you get my drift.

"I don't expect this guy to be wearing a three piece business suit either. Probably a pair of slacks, not pressed very well, a jacket that has been slept in for several days and wearing tennis shoes or sneakers. Maybe a baseball cap pulled down over his forehead. I'm just guessing, of course," said Holder with an air of confidence that came from his experience.

"When we get finished with the cabs let's head over to the food court area. Maybe our man will come to us. I could use a cup of coffee," said Holder's partner.

"Yeah, good idea," said Holder.

The FBI agents went up the escalator to the second level main concourse of the B terminal. They looked in different directions at the crowds of passengers milling through the terminal dragging luggage on little wheels or riding the jitneys through the large aisles. As they arrived the food court, Holder said, "Let me have another look at those pictures of this Russian dude. I want to get his face locked into my mind. It's your turn to buy coffee. Go get some and I'll find a table in the corner."

Bruslov got out of the cab and headed directly to the departure board that listed the next flights to New York City. USAirways flight 77 was scheduled to leave Charlotte in three hours. It was on time and no delays were noted on the board. Everything seemed to be running smoothly. Bruslov went to a kiosk that sold candy, books, souvenirs and newspapers. He purchased several items and stuffed them into his carry-on bag. If the security personnel chose to search his bag he thought these items would help him appear normal and pass as a traveler on a pleasure trip. He could always say the items were for a lady friend in New York City.

Bruslov didn't like the three hour delay and felt uneasy hanging around the airport in the passenger lounge. Security screening officers could become suspicious, check him out and not believe his answers to their questions. The flight to Boston had a longer waiting time. The airport suddenly was becoming risky and there was too much time to kill before the New York City flight departure. He reminded himself, "A moving target is hard to hit. Keep moving and don't wait for the police to become suspicious and check you out."

Bruslov decided his disguise had suited him long enough. He headed for the men's restroom. Before entering the restroom he took extra time and checked for any security officer who might be watching the comings and goings of the men. Nothing seemed out of order. Bruslov entered the men's room and looked for a corner stall. He figured it would take fifteen minutes to freshen up and complete his change of appearance. Afterward he would go to the USAirways ticket counter.

Tilghman was hard at work behind his desk in the Old Executive Office Building on the White House compound. His secretary buzzed his intercom.

"Sara Diamond is on line two. She has fresh news from the CP of Operation Blue Shield."

Tilghman was pressing to stay on top of the rapid developments in Savannah. Presidential advisors and political wonks in the White House were demanding more informations to keep the President in the loop.

"George, I just finished talking with Iron Hand. They have a fix on the terrorist who worked on the bomb. Appears to be some Russian recruited in London and flown over here to build a bomb from what ever they pulled out of the sea near Savannah. We have an APB out for him on the Eastern seaboard. He's on the loose with a four or five hour head start, as best as they can tell at this point."

"What about the others?" asked Tilghman.

"We only know that they are on a power boat somewhere near Tybee Island and Iron Hand's zeroed in on them. No one is in custody so far. Things are looking good but we're not out of the woods yet," said Diamond.

"Sara, if Iron Hand pulls this off, the President will promote him to Rear Admiral the next day. It's too early to start drinking champagne, but we can certainly put some on ice," said Tilghman.

"Not a problem, boss. I'll handle all the party details," said Diamond. She put the phone down and looked at her notes. She thought to herself, "I hope we're not getting too far ahead of ourselves." She searched her index cards for the telephone number of everyone's favorite restaurant in Alexandria, Landini Brothers.

Agent Holder sipped his coffee and said to his partner, "At least we're not dealing with an artist's composite. With a real picture we can actually look through the crowds and hope of making a connection. According to this rap sheet the Russian's name is Sergi Bruslov."

"Sounds like he could play hockey in the NHL for the Detroit Red Wings," said Holder's partner.

"When we finish this coffee, let's visit the men's room. Maybe we'll pass our man in the concourse," said Holder.

"I've got a hunch to play. What's the next flight to New York City? Let's drift over to the passenger gate and see what we come-up with. Just maybe, our man is sitting near the gate trying to act normal and blend into the crowd of passengers. We'll walk over there separately and hang around like we're going to board the plane," said Holder.

"The next flight to New York City is USAirways 77, Terminal B, gate 26," said Holder's partner.

After ten minutes of sitting and watching crowds of passengers walk by gate 26, Holder switched his position to get away from the CNN television screen. He was tired of listening to the same old recycled news.

Holder looked around for his partner. He finally spotted him about fifty feet away giving him a signal that he was on to someone in the crowd. Holder casually worked his way around toward his partner when he saw their man sitting next to some students.

Holder used his cell phone to call for the airport security and police for back-up. They responded in five minutes and were staked-out at each door in the gate area. All escape avenues were closed off if their man attempted to make a run for it.

Holder and his partner moved in for a positive ID. This was their man. Holder spoke first,

"Freeze Bruslov. FBI. Don't make a move. You're under arrest."

The airport police rushed the scene and hand cuffed Bruslov. They then lead him away with any resistance.

Chapter XIV

Iron Hand felt better about the mission progress except that his navy buddy, Paulson, was alone in the Wassaw Sound tailing the terrorist boat and he was stuck in a cinder-covered parking lot. Iron Hand looked at his FBI agent and said,

"How much longer until the chopper with the platoon of marines gets here to secure this area?"

"The chopper pilot confirms he is nearby and has our building in sight," replied the FBI agent. Iron Hand pounded his fist into his palm.

"All right," said Iron Hand; he thought what he really needed was a fresh chopper full of fuel to take him out to Wassaw Sound. Iron Hand told the FBI agent to order the second Coast Guard cutter into Wassaw Sound.

"Have the second cutter tail Game Bird and the terrorist boat; advise the cutter skipper I'll come aboard by a chopper to direct operations against the terrorists."

With three hours showing on the bomb count down device Iron Hand began to wonder if the bomb squad could disarm the bomb so he could stop worrying about an accidental detonation. What if the count down clock mechanism was inaccurate? What if there were only minutes until it exploded. Maybe he should order the entire apparatus flown out to sea immediately? Would the bomb be so unstable that a bumpy flight might set it off? Something told Iron Hand that time was running out. Iron Hand ran into the warehouse and grabbed the nearest bomb technician,

"What's taking so long for you guys to neutralize this thing? Come on, talk to me. I'm starting to get nervous about all this delay."

The bomb squad leader looked at Iron Hand and said, "Hang in there, Captain. We have to do this job right. Everything at this point is under control. We can't afford to cut a corner and mess up now."

Iron Hand knew the man was correct. He backed off and headed out the door to the parking lot.

The thumping beat of the helicopter blades drowned out everything as the chopper landed in the parking lot. Cinders and dirt flew into the air. People had to shield their eyes. The Marine platoon leader signaled an A-OK to Iron Hand.

The Marines immediately secured the area. Rifles were drawn up, loaded and ready for any resistance from inside the warehouse. The Savannah police SWAT team withdrew to their black van and began packing up to leave. Iron Hand knew the Marines could handle any contingency that might occur from this point. It was time for him to get moving after the terrorists in the waters near Tybee Island.

Iron Hand walked up to the chopper cockpit; the pilot sat calmly reviewing the instrument gauges of his machine, its rotor blades idling effortlessly awaiting its next set of orders.

"How much fuel do you have left? Can you get me to a Coast Guard cutter in Wassaw Sound?"

"No problem getting there, Sir. Coming back home might give us a thrill."

Iron Hand thought that Paulson could pick up the chopper pilot if he was forced to ditch, but said nothing.

Iron Hand was ready to get moving, but then thought perhaps he might need some extra fire power from a few marines.

"Lieutenant, can you spare three riflemen for a trip with me? Make sure they know how to swim."

"Yes sir. "Beyers, Scott and Groves. Go with the Captain. Can all of you swim?"

Three "Yes, Sirs" came right back in unison. Iron Hand and his three Marine riflemen boarded the chopper. Adrenaline caused their hearts to beat faster.

"OK skipper. Head out over Wassaw Sound. I'm looking for a forty-three foot Sabreliner and a thirty-eight foot Sea Ray one-a-half miles behind on the same southerly course. Speed about eighteen knots. Show me what you can do," said Iron Hand. The Marine chopper jumped into the air and flew over the trees that lined Victory Road. One could only imagine what civilians might have thought at at this sight. What kind of a Marine drill would be scheduled for a neighborhood?

After ten minutes, the picture seemed clearer to Iron Hand; He had three F-18's orbiting three miles out at 5,000 feet and a Coast Guard cutter closing on the terrorists at full speed. It appeared the cutter would be alongside Paulson in eight minutes.

"Skipper, can you get the four of us aboard that cutter just ahead?"

"Shouldn't be a problem in these waters, Captain."

"Radio them you have four men that must come aboard immediately."

*   *   *   *

Ahmad and Omar were starting to sweat and it showed. Ahmad kept checking his watch, hoping his bomb would soon detonate. Abdul was a total wreck. He was ready to end it all by jumping overboard. They pressed on at full throttle but, at this rate their fuel would be consumed in one hour. Ahmad had decided that he would not be taken alive. He thought of ramming the Coast Guard cutter in a glorious crash to kill more Americans. Omar could help him. Abdul could jump into the water if he so chose.

"Slow down a little. Let the Americans come closer," said Ahmad to Omar. Ahmad thought he could save some fuel and perhaps sink the cutter.

*   *   *   *

The Marine chopper hovered over the cutter. The three Marines dropped down first with their weapons. Iron Hand followed. A piece of cake. The chopper broke off and headed back to the warehouse; its fuel remaining was low, but it was probably enough to get home. Maybe a ditching wouldn't be necessary.

Once onboard the cutter, Iron Hand told the skipper, a young ensign, he was taking over operational command. The ensign agreed that was a good idea.

"What is our fuel situation, skipper?"

"We have enough fuel for three hours of chasing this boat, Sir."

"Very well." said Iron Hand. "It appears we are overtaking them now. Have they backed off a little?"

"Yes sir, I noticed that too. They may get cute and try to play some tricks on us."

"Like what?" asked Iron Hand.

"They could turn that boat on a dime and try to ram us if we get too close."

Iron Hand surveyed the situation from the cutter's bridge. "Do we have radio contact with our F-18 fighter CAP?"

"Yes, sir. Punch in the third panel button and speak directly to the F-18 flight leader." said the cutter's skipper.

"Flight Leader. This is Iron Hand on the cutter below you. Give the boat ahead of us a low level fly-by at one hundred feet. We will have Marines to suppress any small arms fire directed at you from the vessel."

"Iron Hand from Flight leader. We have you in sight. Commencing our low level run now." Iron Hand ordered the Marines forward to stand by to deliver covering fire. Iron Hand shouted to the Marines,

"If anyone on the vessel ahead raises a gun to shoot at our jets, your job is to shoot to kill." The Marines jumped to Iron Hand's order. They loaded and locked up with ammunition. They signaled a thumbs-up, OK back to Iron Hand.

The distance to Serious Business was now less than 150 yards. From this distance it would be hard to miss anyone aboard Serious Business. A Marine rifleman shooting from this distance would call the targets, "duck soup."

The F-18's thundered by overhead with a deafening roar, enough to scare the most ardent terrorist. Anyone normal would start waving a white flag, but there was no movement by anyone aboard Serious Business. The Marines appeared to be disappointed that they weren't able to prove their marksmanship. Suddenly there was movement aboard Serious Business. Someone was jumping overboard. Yes, one terrorist was overboard, swimming for his life. Iron Hand grabbed the bull horn loud speaker and yelled,

"Throw two life rings overboard and a smoke marker as we pass the man in the sea." As the cutter raced by the man in the water a lookout reported the swimmer had reached a life ring.

*　　　　*　　　　*　　　　*

Omar and Ahmad watched in disbelief when Abdul left their boat after the jets low level fly-by. Ahmad figured his brother was in the hands of Allah now.

"The stupid Americans have taken our bait," said Ahmad to Omar. Abdul has unwittingly given us another chance. They now think we are afraid. Slow down a little more. At one hundred yards we will swing the boat around for a direct collision course to the cutter. Once we turn, go to full throttle. The faster we are going, the bigger the hole we make in their vessel."

*　　　　*　　　　*　　　　*

The young skipper turned to Iron Hand. "Captain, I don't like this. Can we throw a few shots into their stern to slow them down. Maybe bust up their rudder or screws. We're getting too close for comfort and we have no back-up."

"You're right, skipper." said Iron Hand.

Iron Hand raced to the front of the bridge and shouted orders for the Marines to open fire on the stern; aim at the water line, slow down Serious Business and maybe knock out an engine or damage the rudder.

*   *   *   *

Ahmad yelled at Omar, "Swing around sharply and ram them, now!" As the boat swung on its axis the Marines opened fire. Most of their shots were high and wide. A few hit the rear transom and tore up the guardrail. Omar knew what he was doing. He swung Serious Business into a perfect collision course and accelerated to full rpm's. The distance between the two vessels now was less than sixty yards and closing rapidly. The cutter's skipper reacted;

"Stand by to turn to port, on my command," shouted the Ensign. By attempting to avoid a direct collision and settle for a glancing blow this would minimized damage to both vessels. There would be no worry about his cutter ever sinking. The terrorist's boat however, could certainly sink after this tactical maneuver.

Iron Hand grabbed a bull horn and yelled to the Marines, "Shoot to kill at their bridge." The Marines opened up with their rifles but it was too late to stop Serious Business. Omar's only interest was killing everyone on board the cutter.

The cutter's skipper sounded the collision alarm for the men below deck.

The collision sounded like two eighteen wheelers bouncing off each other on I-95. Omar was at the helm of Serious Business but mortally wounded. He had slumped to the deck after the collision, his head a mass of bruises and cuts around the eyes. Ahmad was hiding in the lower cabin,

165

alive and well but shaken by the collision. Majed was lying on the deck near the wheel, bleeding and mortally wounded.

Iron Hand stood on the cutter's main deck. His nine millimeter pistol armed, safety off, and the trigger lock set for full automatic fire. Iron Hand saw Omar and Majed lying near death by the wheel. As Iron Hand prepared to go aboard, he ordered two marines to follow. The third marine stayed on the cutter to give them cover.

Iron Hand jumped from the cutter and signaled to the marines to follow. Iron Hand started his move toward the forward cabin when he heard a voice,

"Looking for me, you American dog?"

Iron Hand swung around to confront Ahmad not more than six feet away. He raised his gun to fire a shot but Ahmad had already started his forward lunging leap to grab Iron Hand. Ahmad kicked Iron Hand's right hand and his pistol fired twice into the air and dropped to the deck with a thud.

"Now we fight to the death, man to man, you American dog." said Ahmad.

Iron Hand was sick of hearing this and retorted, "You Islamic bastards all stink. Take this." Iron Hand loaded up his right hand and punched at Ahmad's face. He saw the blow coming and was able to dodge most of the punch. Iron Hand's powerful fist glanced off Ahmad's ear and drew blood. They grabbed at each other and rolled to the deck. Iron Hand landed several hard body blows and Ahmad started to go down. Iron Hand loaded up his right hand again but Ahmad gave Iron Hand a quick kick in the knee. Iron Hand went down on one leg. He felt a little dizzy and struggled up to defend himself. Ahmad found a piece of metal transom and was making ready to smash Iron Hand in the face.

With what little strength Iron Hand had left, he dodged left, slammed into Ahmad's legs and came up like a NFL defensive lineman rolling up the offensive line on the goal line. Ahmad's blow with the metal transom missed Iron Hand's head and hit the railing behind him with a loud clank. Now Ahmad was on the deck and Iron Hand was pinning him down with his body. Ahmad's head had bounced off the deck of Serious Business and he was slightly dazed. Several fast right hand blows to the head by Iron Hand and Ahmad was out cold. Blood was running from one eye.

"Nice job, Captain. Are you an experienced bar fighter?' asked Marine corporal Scott, who had been standing a few paces from the fight. Iron Hand looked back and said,

"Where were you when I needed you?"

"Well, sir, you seemed to be doing OK. I didn't want to stop all your fun. We enlisted people don't actually get to see many Navy Captains in hand-to-hand bar fights."

"Is this guy dead?" asked Marine corporal Groves, looking at Ahmad.

"I certainly hope so," replied Iron Hand.

Iron Hand backed off a few paces and attempted to catch his breath. "Get over here and check these guys out. Make sure they are dead or tied up and ready for the ride back to shore."

"Secure this boat for a tow back to the Wilmington River. All three of you will remain on board to guard the terrorists. If one of them comes to and causes any trouble; you have my permission to smack them," said Iron Hand.

"Yes Sir. Nice job, Captain, Sir," said a Marine private Beyers.

The cutter took Serious Business in tow and retraced its course back toward the Wilmington River. Iron Hand finally got a breather and was happy the ordeal was over. As the cutter came up along side Paulson in Game Bird, they slowed and fished Abdul out of the water. Paulson had Abdul covered with his .45 Colt. The Marine finally got him tied up. He was placed on Serious Business under guard with the other terrorists. Ahmad was unconscious; barely breathing. Iron Hand yelled over to Paulson,

"Deane, follow us back to the Wilmington River. We'll dock at the shrimp pier across from Tubby's. Can you handle that? If anyone asks about all this activity just say this was a drug bust." As the boats made their way back to the shrimp pier, Iron Hand thought he heard Victory at Sea music coming over the waves from Game Bird.

Iron Hand dialed the cell phone numbers to his Command Post communication center at Hunter Army Airfield. "Patch me up to my office in Langley," said Iron Hand. In a few seconds he heard Sara's voice,

"Iron Hand, how is everything going? Everyone is very nervous and dying for the latest news up-date."

"There is good news to report. "Operation Blue Shield is complete. The Islamic terrorists are in my custody or dead. The bomb is being transferred to a cutter ten miles out in the gulf stream for further study and will be rendered totally harmless.

I expect to be here a few days to clean up some details before heading home. I'll get back to you later today," said Iron Hand.

"This is great news. The DCI says he is going to recommend you for promotion to Admiral, in the Confederate Navy. The FBI in Charlotte just reported they have a Russian in custody who matches the photo of Sergi Bruslov. Catch you later. Don't be a stranger," said Sara.

As the cutter approached the dock he could see a crowd of people beginning to grow. Obviously someone had alerted the local media; Iron Hand could see sound trucks, TV cameras and reporters filming background for the evening news. A small television news helicopter flew overhead and he clearly saw the sign TV22 designation . A reporter was hanging precariously out of the helicopter as she attempted to get pictures. He scanned the crowd for Sherry and found her near the ramp leading up from the shrimp dock. The crowd had no clue what had transpired in the Wassaw Sound.

After a few questions from Coast Guard officials and the local police, Iron Hand told the Marines to place the terrorists into a van for transfer to Hunter Army Airfield. Iron Hand planned to have them flown out of Savannah to avoid any paper work entanglements with the local police or the Georgia State legal system.

Iron Hand finally caught up with Sherry after a few more few questions from the local media. Iron Hand wasn't compelled to tell the media there had been a terrorist nuclear bomb threat because they didn't know enough to ask the right questions. His old buddy Paulson seemed to like all the media attention. He was heard to say,

"I just happened to be in the area and decided to lend a helping hand to the Coast Guard. I'm no hero. Just an alert good citizen."

Iron Hand looked at Sherry and said, "How about dinner tonight?"

Sherry shrugged her shoulders and answered, "I told you before, I'm a sucker for a military guy in a uniform."

"Let's start off with a drink at Tubby's. I'll figure out some other place for dinner and after that, let's see where we go from there," said Iron Hand.

Sherry smiled and then hooked her hand around Iron Hand's sore body. They walked up the old shrimp pier to Tubby's arm in arm.

After Iron Hand finished his first drink with Sherry, he asked her to order another round and excused himself to visit the men's room. As soon as he cleared the door and locked it, he called his Command Post. He asked for a report on his message traffic.

"Captain, your voice-mail message box is full and will not accept more traffic. We are hand writing your new messages on paper for review upon your return."

Iron Hand acknowledged the command post communication watch officer and said,

"Take this down. This is important. Have two FBI agents clean out my room at the BOQ. Get me a two-room suite at the Lafayette Arms Square hotel in downtown Savannah. Move all my personal belonging there. Also, make dinner reservations for two in the main dining room for 8:00pm. I will handle everything from there. Get back to me when this is all handled."

Iron Hand thought to himself: now that everything is wrapped up except for the paper work, I want to stay at a decent hotel. The watch officer said,

"Yes, sir, Captain. I will personally see to this order."

Iron Hand cut the circuit on the cell phone and replaced it in his pocket. He thought he had spent enough time in the BOQ and deserved a break after risking his life foiling the terrorist plot. Now back to Sherry, Iron Hand told himself,

"There was a good chance that something big might come up this evening." When Iron Hand got back to the table Sherry greeted him with a big smile.

"I'm staying at the Lafayette Arms Square hotel for the next two evenings. How about dinner tonight at 8:00pm. Can we meet there?" said Iron Hand.

"Wild horses couldn't keep me from being there," said Sherry.

* * * *

Iron Hand put down his glass of wine and looked into Sherry's eyes. "I'm afraid I may have ruined any plans you had with Abdul." Sherry sighed and said,

"Abdul and I had an adult relationship but I wasn't emotionally involved with him. I realized our relationship would never become permanent. Actually, I was beginning to think he was acting a little strange. I had no idea that he was helping a ring of terrorist bomb plotters. What will happen to him now?"

Iron Hand decided there was no need to hit her too hard with the truth, so he attempted to soft pedal his answer. "He will probably go to jail but if he decides to cooperate with the investigation, he might get a reduced sentence. His brother will never be walking free on the streets again."

Sherry seemed to take this information in stride. She dropped her eyes and stared at her glass of wine. After gathering her thoughts, she looked up at Iron Hand,

"What about you? When will you be leaving Savannah? Will I ever hear from you again after tonight?"

Iron Hand looked straight back at Sherry and said, "I'll be going to Washington in a few days. I don't know why we can't stay in touch. Sometimes things have a way of working out for the best." Iron Hand was glad to see the waiter coming to the table. Their conversation was moving along a little too fast.

"May I show you the menu for the evening meal?" said the waiter in a polite southern manner. "Yes, that would be fine. And please bring each of us another glass of Merlot," answered Iron Hand.

Iron Hand surveyed the black leather bound menu: Crown Roast Lamb, Broiled Long Island Duckling, Baked Bourbon-Glazed Southern Ham, Southern Fried Chicken in Cream Gravy and stuffed Pork Chops. Side dishes of grits and cheddar cheese casserole accompanied all the entrees. Fresh garden salads and toasted parmesan & garlic dressing. Southern Pecan Pie and Black Coffee were the suggested finishing touches to all the dinners.

Sherry offered, "I haven't seen such a delightful menu in ages. I'm sure that any of these selections would be just fine. Why don't you order something for me. You can surprise me. I like surprises."

Iron Hand scanned the menu and ordered Crown Roast Lamb for Sherry and he chose the Pork Chops with southern sausage meat, bread crumbs, thyme, chopped parsley topped with freshly ground pepper, chopped onions and carrots seasoned with thyme.

Iron Hand hoped that just maybe Sherry could surprise him later. As the meal wound down and the small talk subsided, Sherry said, "I've never been here. I've always

172

wondered about the rooms. Would you like to show me your room?"

Iron Hand gathered himself. This was turning out better than he could have even imagined. He signaled for the check, computed a nice tip, and charged the dinner to his room. They left the dining room holding hands and walked directly to the elevator. Once in the room Sherry walked toward the windows and exclaimed,

"What a beautiful view of Savannah." She kicked off her shoes and turned and looked into Iron Hand's eyes. Iron Hand pulled her near and whispered,

"I like a woman who knows what she wants."

*   *   *   *